Accidentally Fooled

candy apple books...
just for you.
sweet. fresh. fun.
take a bite!

The Accidental Cheerleader by Mimi McCoy

The Boy Next Door by Laura Dower

Miss Popularity by Francesco Sedita

How to Be a Girly Girl in Just Ten Days
by Lisa Papademetriou

Drama Queen by Lara Bergen

The Babysitting Wars by Mimi McCoy

Totally Crushed by Eliza Willard

I've Got a Secret by Lara Bergen

Callie for President by Robin Wasserman

Making Waves by Randi Reisfeld and H. B. Gilmour

The Sister Switch
by Jane B. Mason and Sarah Hines Stephens

Accidentally Fabulous by Lisa Papademetriou

Confessions of a Bitter Secret Santa by Lara Bergen

Accidentally Famous by Lisa Papademetriou

Star-Crossed by Mimi McCoy

by Lisa Papademetriou

SCHOLASTIC INC.

New York Toronto London Auckland Sydney
Mexico City New Delhi Hong Kong Buenos Aires

For Deena Bakri, Bethel McCoy, Johanna Jones, and all other Lanier Middle School students, past, present, and future

ISBN-13: 978-0-545-05582-6
ISBN-10: 0-545-05582-2

12 11 10 9 8 7 6 5 4 3 2 1 9 10 11 12 13 14/0
Printed in the U.S.A.
First printing, April 2009

CHAPTER ONE

Health Hint: Hearts beat roughly 100,000 times a day. (Maybe more, if you're crushing really hard.)

"You can see the whole school from up here," I said as I gazed down from the top of the Ferris wheel. A carnival spread out below us, sprawling across the lush green Allington Academy campus. It was completely amazing. Loud music blared from a nearby stage, where bands were scheduled to appear all day. There were tons of cool rides and games — the school had even set up an enormous half-pipe for skateboarders. "Can you believe how many people showed up? It's so great that the school invites the whole neighborhood to this!"

"Just tell me when we're back on the ground." My good friend Kiwi Adair had her eyes squeezed tight.

"Okay," I said.

"Oh, phew," Kiwi said, opening her eyes. She let out a shriek when she saw that we were still practically scraping the sky. "That was so mean! I can't believe you did that to me!" She reached for the plastic water pistol on the seat beside her and gave me a playful squirt. "You're pure evil, Amy Flowers!"

I squirted her back. "I *meant* 'Okay, I'll let you know,' not 'Okay, ride's over.'"

Our car, which was stopped at the top of the wheel, rocked as we moved. Kiwi gave another shriek. "I can't believe you even got me to go on this ride in the first place! You know I'm afraid of heights!"

"What?" I spluttered as a series of short blasts of water hit me in the face. "You're the one who talked *me* into this!" Laughing, I landed a few squirts along her ear and in her long auburn hair. We'd won the squirt guns playing a ring-toss game, and I actually didn't mind getting wet. It was March and already hot in Houston. The water and the air at the top of the Ferris wheel were refreshing.

"You should have known I was talking crazy!"

Kiwi insisted. She yelped as the wheel gave a lurch and began to glide toward Earth. Kiwi's long tie-dyed sundress fluttered in the breeze as she screamed all the way down.

As we floated down toward the waiting line, someone shouted, "That's why you shouldn't let girls go on a Ferris wheel!" Preston Harringford grinned up at me. He was standing beside the metal gate, next in line. "They'll break your eardrums!"

The wheel was still turning. Without thinking, I reached out and squirted him in the face with my water pistol just as we passed him.

The Ferris wheel pulled us up and into the sky, but not before I caught a glimpse of Preston's expression: He was shocked, amused, and — probably for the first time in history — speechless.

In the car beside me, Kiwi's screams had turned to laughter. "Omigosh," she said, giggling. "Did you see his face? That was priceless!" She held up her hand and I gave her a high five.

The Ferris wheel stopped again. This time, we were about halfway down. "This isn't so bad," Kiwi said slowly. "Look! Is that Mitchie on the half-pipe?"

"I think so," I said as a figure in a pink helmet hopped onto a skateboard and took the sickening plunge down the U-shaped ramp. Our good friend Michiko Ohara swooshed to the top and seemed to hang in the air as she twisted one and a half times before plummeting toward the wooden half-pipe.

The Ferris wheel started up again, and we coasted back toward the ground. “Oh, no!” I exclaimed.

“What?” Kiwi leaned forward so she could see what I was looking at. It was Preston. He was waiting for us in the same spot we’d left him.

And he had a *bucket*.

Kiwi and I shrieked as a tidal wave landed over our heads, completely drenching us.

“Gotcha!” Preston called after us as we soared back into the air.

Kiwi was laughing so hard that she could hardly catch her breath.

“I guess I should’ve thought about the fact that we’d have to go past him again,” I said sheepishly as water dripped down my face. But I was giggling, too. Preston had gotten me good that time. He drove me crazy, but he could also be funny.

“Oh, who cares?” Kiwi flicked her long, wet hair out of her face. “It feels good.”

My brown-and-pink sundress was stuck to my body. I peeled it from my skin, and it ballooned outward as the Ferris wheel made its final descent.

Preston was long gone by the time we got out of the car. Oh, well. My squirt gun was out of ammo, anyway.

"What next?" Kiwi twisted her long hair into a knot and tied it at the nape of her neck. I wished I could do that. My hair was still wet, but half of it was already turning into a frizzball in the Houston sun. "Gravitron?" She pointed to a ride that spun you around at about a zillion miles per hour.

"If I go on that thing, I'll be wearing the cotton candy I just ate," I told her.

"Gross!" Kiwi replied just as a voice behind me said, "Hey, Amy."

Turning, I found myself looking directly into a familiar pair of deep-brown eyes. It was Scott Lawton, and he was smiling at me as he took a sip of the soda in his hand. "I like your hair," he said. He was teasing, of course, but his voice wasn't mean.

"Oh, yeah — the wet look is really in." Giggling nervously, I grabbed my hair into a ponytail and tried to twist it into something other than a cotton ball.

"So I see," Scott said, smiling at Kiwi. "What do you think of this year's carnival?"

"Oh, it's great," Kiwi gushed. "Step Out is the best."

Step Out is Allington Academy's community service project. All the seventh and eleventh graders spend half of the school day working for a local organization. The school always kicks off the two weeks of work with a carnival.

"Do you know what you're doing yet?" Scott asked. He was in eighth grade, so it wasn't his year to volunteer.

"We're supposed to find out Tuesday," I explained. "There's a presentation on Monday, and then we decide what we want to do." I felt a little weird around Scott. For a while, I'd thought that we were kind of going out. But lately I wasn't sure. . . .

"What did you do last year?" Kiwi asked.

"Soup kitchen," Scott said. "It was cool." He ran a hand through his sandy-blond hair, which was gleaming in the sun. He'd clearly never worried about frizz in his life.

"Hey, Scott!" A guy I didn't know waved from the front of the Gravitron line. "Hurry up, man, or you'll lose your spot!"

"Gotta go," Scott said, draining the last of his soda. He dropped it into a trash can and trotted toward his friend, then suddenly stopped. "Hey,

Amy," he said, turning around. "Listen, my dad's company designed this new video game, and they're having a big party to celebrate. It's in a week. Do you want to come?"

With a little squeal, Kiwi kicked me in the ankle. I love her, but she's not too good at playing it cool.

"Sure," I said. "That would be great."

"Oh, but — it's kind of a fancy party." Scott held out his hands apologetically. "You'll have to get dressed up."

"Amy doesn't mind," Kiwi said eagerly.

I flashed her a warning look. "I don't mind."

"Great!" Scott grinned. "Excellent!"

"Scott, come on!" his friend urged. The line was starting to move.

"You'd better go," I told him.

"Right. Okay. See you!" He ran off, disappearing into the mass of people making their way onto the Gravitron.

"Oooooooooo," Kiwi sang, elbowing me in the ribs. "Someone has a date!"

"You think?" I asked. I felt a blush rising to my cheeks and hoped Scott couldn't see me from the whirling Gravitron. When I blush, my face turns bright red, with a weird little white blotch in the center of each cheek. Given my damp dress and my hair's frizz factor, I wasn't exactly looking like Miss America.

"It's definitely a date!" Kiwi smiled, her brown eyes dancing. "It's for a Saturday night, isn't it? It's to a red-carpet party, right?"

I shrugged as Kiwi and I fell into step, heading toward the half-pipe. "Sounds like it."

"I'll help you find the perfect thing to wear," Kiwi promised. "And Mitchie can help with your hair — she's really good at that stuff."

"She is?" I asked. Somehow, I didn't see my tomboy skater friend having a talent for hairstyles.

"Didn't you know?" Kiwi asked. "Pick any cool style out of a magazine, Mitchie can do it."

"What can I do?" Mitchie asked, walking up to us. She was smiling, her pink helmet tucked under her elbow. She shook her bobbed black hair, which fell perfectly into place.

"I was just explaining to Amy that you're the Hairstyle Queen," Kiwi said. "She's got a date with Scott Lawton."

"Way to go," Mitchie said, waggling her eyebrows.

"I'm not sure it's a date," I told her.

"It's a date," Kiwi said.

"If you need a cool hairstyle, it's a date," Mitchie agreed.

I decided to change the subject. "We saw you on the half-pipe from the top of the Ferris wheel. Awesome moves."

"I came down a little hard on that three-sixty," Mitchie said modestly. "I thought I'd fall off. Hey, by the way, your brother was about to go down the half-pipe just a minute ago."

"He was?" I was surprised. Kirk isn't exactly talented with a skateboard. I turned to look and saw a tall guy limping toward us. It was kind of funny to see my brother at my school. He goes to the public high school about half a mile away and usually calls the Allington kids "private school snobs." "How'd it go?" I called cheerfully.

Kirk glared at me. "I fell."

"At least you weren't hurt," Mitchie said, giving him a sympathetic smile.

"I've got skid marks on my arm from where three guys ran over me," Kirk told her.

"At least you weren't hurt *badly*," I offered. Kirk smacked me playfully on the head, and I tried to squirt him with my empty water pistol.

"How do you do it, Mitchie?" Kirk demanded. "You're so smooth up there. You just —" He made a loop-de-loop with his hand. "It's like you're floating! You make it look so easy!"

Mitchie blushed, turning pink all the way to her nose. It was cute on *her*. When I blush, it looks like I've got bull's-eyes painted on my cheeks. "I just practice a lot," she admitted.

"Well, maybe you could help me out a little sometime," Kirk said.

"Okay, sure!" Mitchie said quickly. "No problem. Anytime!"

"He could use it," I put in.

"All right." Kirk sighed. "I guess I'll give the half-pipe one more try before I head home. Might as well take advantage of this fancy school while they're letting riffraff like me in." He gave us a wink and walked back to the half-pipe.

"You're not riffraff!" Mitchie called, but Kirk was out of earshot.

Kiwi gave her a look.

It took Mitchie a moment to notice. "What?" she asked.

Kiwi glanced at me, then back at Mitchie. Finally, she shook her head. "Nothing," she said.

But she didn't need to say anything — I'd already read her mind. It was starting to look suspiciously like Mitchie had a little crush on Kirk. My *brother*!

I'd never even realized that was *possible*. I mean, okay, he has cute shaggy brown hair and usually smells decent. And he's a nice guy — some of the time. But he trims his toenails over the wastebasket in the middle of the living room! Who could have a crush on a guy like that?

The thought gave me a strange feeling in my stomach. Would it be freaky for my friend to go out with my brother? I snuck a sideways look at Mitchie, who was watching as Kirk dropped in on the half-pipe.

"Whoa!" he cried as he flailed toward the bottom. "Whoa-oa-oa!"

Mitchie winced. "Ouch," she said as he landed on his backside.

No doubt about it — they would definitely be one seriously weird couple.

"Did you guys look at the catalog?" Kiwi asked as we settled into the cushy oversized seats in the Allington auditorium on Monday. She was holding a glossy brochure with a bright red cover and the words STEP OUT! in bold silver letters on the front. "All of the projects look so cool!"

"I looked at it yesterday," I said, flipping through the pages. The volunteer opportunities were explained in detail, some with photos. "How are we supposed to decide on a project?"

"I didn't even look at the catalog — I already know I want to work in the community garden." Mitchie leaned back in her blue velvet seat.

"Oh, yeah, that sounds amazing!" Kiwi flipped to the page. "Look — they even have a chicken coop!"

"And they run a great compost program," Mitchie said. "They take a huge chunk of the kitchen garbage from the neighborhood and turn it into excellent soil."

"That sounds perfect for you, Mitchie," a snide voice behind us interrupted. "You already know so much about garbage."

Fiona Von Steig's ice-blue eyes glittered at us as she slipped delicately into the seat behind mine. Her good friend Lucia de Leon was right beside her. Together, they made up two-thirds of the League, the Queen Bugs — I mean, Bees — of Allington Academy.

"Yeah," Lucia agreed. "Be careful, or they might, like, put your outfit with the rest of the trash?" Every sentence that came out of Lucia's mouth sounded like a question — even the insulting ones.

"At least my *personality* doesn't belong in the Dumpster," Mitchie shot back.

"Why are you guys so mean all the time?" Kiwi asked Lucia and Fiona. She looked curious, like she was seriously trying to figure it out.

Fiona ignored her. "I saw you on the half-pipe on Saturday," she told Mitchie coolly. "You and the rest of the boys."

Mitchie shrugged.

"You *wish* you could hang out with as many guys as Mitchie does," I said.

"Oh, please." Fiona laughed, tucking her long black hair behind one ear. "At least when I hang out with guys, they don't mistake me for one of them."

"Yeah, because Mitchie dresses like a boy?" Lucia put in. "They're, like, confused?"

"Seriously, Mitchie, you should get with the program," Fiona warned. "Guys don't like girls who are more athletic than they are."

"Really, Fiona?" Mitchie snapped. "Is that what *your* boyfriend says?"

Fiona didn't have a comeback for that one — because she didn't have a boyfriend. Fiona cast a quick glance at Jenelle, who was sitting with Anderson Sempe five rows ahead of us. Jenelle was my friend, even though she was in the League, too. But lately, she'd been spending a lot of time with Anderson. Fiona didn't say anything else. She just sat there with her mouth pursed into a frown as Mitchie turned around in her chair.

"Good one," I whispered to Mitchie as the lights started to go down in the auditorium.

Mitchie nodded a little, but I caught her looking down at her outfit. She had on denim capris and a red tank top with a fierce dragon across the back. Okay, so it wasn't as feminine as the blue halter dress Fiona had on. But it was *her*. I wanted to tell Mitchie that she looked great, but I'd missed my chance — our headmistress had already stepped up to the microphone.

"Good morning, pupils," she said as a giant screen rose from the floor behind her. Headmistress Cardinal had a nice face — round, with lots of wrinkles — surrounded by a helmet of white hair. Whenever I saw her, I thought of Mrs. Claus. "Welcome to this year's Step Out program!"

The auditorium exploded as the seventh grade let out a cheer. "As you know, here at Allington, we believe in educating the whole student," Headmistress Cardinal went on once the place had quieted down. "We believe in honor, excellence, and service." A slide show of Step Out projects from previous years flashed across the screen as she explained how the program worked: Small groups of seventh graders would spend half of every school day working in the community for two weeks. At the end, each group would give a presentation. Our Step Out grade would appear on our report card, and eighty percent of the grade was dependent on the final presentation. Our advisors at the volunteer site would determine the other twenty percent of our grade based on attendance and cooperation.

Then a few people from different community agencies spoke. The man from the soup kitchen talked about the importance of feeding the hungry. He said that in Texas, nearly one in five adults and nearly one in four children have to go without food because they don't have enough money to pay for it. I looked up at the giant crystal chandelier above me. It was suspended from a black ceiling, set with fiber-optic lights that were designed to look like constellations in the southern hemisphere. It was hard to believe that there were hungry people just outside these walls, but I knew it was true.

The woman from the community garden had long gray dreadlocks and wore a flowing purple dress. “We’re planting a tranquillity garden,” she explained. “It’s a place for people to come when they need to get away from the city.” Images of the garden in bloom appeared on the screen behind her. “It’s a place for folks to sit and think — and look at something beautiful.”

Kiwi leaned forward in her chair and flashed Mitchie a smile.

“And now, I’d like you to meet one of our past volunteers,” the headmistress said. “He’s doing a special project with the Health on the Move Experience, which he helped set up when he was in seventh grade. Please welcome Anthony Porter.”

Everyone clapped politely as a tall, good-looking boy with dark-brown skin, large soulful eyes, and a brilliant smile walked up to the podium. Whoa. Anthony Porter was seriously good-looking. I could tell Kiwi thought so, too, because she was kicking my ankle like crazy.

“Thanks, Headmistress Cardinal,” Anthony said into the microphone. He had a smooth voice, like a radio announcer, and I wondered if he’d practiced his speech in the mirror. “I’d like to take a moment to tell you all about the Health on the Move Experience, or HOME. We travel from school to school, teaching about the dangers of smoking and the benefits of a healthy diet and exercise. As you probably know, obesity is becoming a health crisis. . . ." He talked about how important it was to teach kids about exercise and nutrition. I winced a little bit, thinking about all of the time I'd been spending on the couch lately, gobbling Fudge Romance ice cream by the bowlful. Yikes.

"During Step Out, we'll be at McClure Elementary School," Anthony went on. "We'll work with kindergarten through third grades." Images of smiling kids flashed up on the enormous screen behind him. One little boy was jumping rope; a gap-toothed girl grinned as she held up a model lung. "It's important work, but it's fun, too. I hope you'll consider joining me." He flashed that killer smile once more, then stepped back and took his seat on the stage.

There were representatives from a few more volunteer organizations, but I barely heard what they had to say. My mind was made up.

"So," Mitchie said as the lights went up and people began to file out of the auditorium. "Have you guys picked a project?"

"I *still* can't decide," Kiwi wailed.

"I'm thinking Health on the Move," I put in.

"Oh, that's really *cute*," Fiona said from her seat behind me. "Amy thinks she's going to get with Anthony Porter."

"I do not," I snapped.

"Yeah, like, get in line?" Lucia piped up. "I'm pretty sure we're *all* into volunteering with Mr. Hotness, right, Fiona?"

Fiona snorted. "Oh, please," she said. "I wouldn't be caught dead on the moving health wagon. It's more Amy's style — completely ridiculous."

"Seriously?" Lucia's delicate brown eyebrows shot up.

"I'm thinking about the soup kitchen." Fiona pointed to the page in the catalog. "That's what you should do, Lucia. You're good with food. You could do an amazing final project."

Lucia's family owned a chain of restaurants in Houston. "That's true?" she said. "I mean, I could probably get an A?"

"With your brain tied behind your back," Fiona said.

"Thanks, Fiona," Lucia said warmly. It was the first thing she'd said that didn't sound like a question.

I guess life is pretty easy when you have Fiona to tell you what to do all of the time, I thought.

Fiona flashed me a smug smile as the two of them walked off together.

Whatever — I didn't care what Fiona thought about the Health on the Move Experience. I was still going to volunteer. And if she thought it was ridiculous, even better.

At least that way I wouldn't be stuck on a health van with the meanest girl at Allington Academy.

CHAPTER TWO

Health Hint: Human intestines are about twenty-seven feet long. (Ewwwwwww!)

"Where are you?" I muttered to myself as I searched one of the many pockets in my new handbag. I'd gotten it as a gift for helping organize a fashion show — and I loved it. Deep-orange suede and covered in pockets, it was the prettiest bag I'd ever owned. "There you are!" I pulled the pen and my small homework notebook from one of the fashionable outside pockets. You'd think my notebook wouldn't be that hard to find — it was bright purple and had a blue monkey on the front — but that was the drawback of having so many compartments. I checked my homework list and started pulling books from my locker.

"Nice handbag," Fiona said as she walked up behind me. "Where'd you get it — Pockets R Us?"

But I didn't even need to think of a witty reply, because Jenelle was with her. "That's an Adelaide Fromm bag, isn't it?" she asked, reaching out to touch it. "Soft as feathers." Her fingers lingered over the deep-orange suede. "Mom carries these at Bounce." Bounce was the trendiest store in Houston, and Jenelle's mother owned it.

Fiona glowered. "Why do you need so many pockets, Amy?" she asked, folding her arms across her chest. "You don't even have a cell phone."

"No, but she's got everything else," Jenelle said playfully. She likes to tease me about all of the stuff I haul around in my purse. "Which reminds me . . ." Jenelle peeked into her tiny wristlet and pulled out a pale peach envelope the size of a credit card. My name was written on the front in brown calligraphy. "I've got something for you."

"What is it?" I asked as I flipped over the envelope. It had a wax seal with a raised flower pattern. Schmancy.

"It's an invitation to my mom's wedding shower," Jenelle explained. "It's Wednesday night. Your mom's already invited, but I was hoping you could come, too, to keep me company."

"Oh, right — I think my mom mentioned it." Jenelle's mom was getting married to my uncle Steve in a few weeks, so our family was invited to all of the wedding stuff. I tucked the invitation into one of my bag's five zillion pockets, telling myself I'd open it later. I couldn't bear to break that pretty seal just yet.

"Where's *my* invitation?" Fiona demanded.

"You want to come?" Jenelle's hazel eyes widened in surprise. "I mean, it's just going to be a bunch of my mom's friends sitting around and opening presents." Her long blond hair was tied back in a bun, and she touched it nervously.

Fiona just gave her a lifted-eyebrow look.

"I — I'm sorry," Jenelle stammered. "But we're kind of just inviting family."

I couldn't help smiling a little.

"Amy isn't your family," Fiona shot back. "Steve isn't even her real uncle!"

This is technically true. Uncle Steve is actually my dad's best friend. But Uncle Steve doesn't have any brothers or sisters, and I know he thinks of me and Kirk as his niece and nephew. I was positive that he had asked Linda to invite me.

"I'll ask my mom," Jenelle said quickly.

"Gee, *thanks*." Fiona's voice was sarcastic. "But, like, no big deal. We don't have to do everything together, right? I mean, Lucia and I are going to La Luxe spa this afternoon to get pedicures, and we didn't invite you to *that*."

I was pretty sure that Fiona had just come up with that story about the spa on the spot, but it didn't faze Jenelle at all. "Oh, that's okay," she said. "I've got plans with Anderson, anyway."

Fiona's face darkened, and Anderson picked that perfect moment to appear. "Hey, Jenelle!" he said, his bright blue eyes shining. "Ready to go? Hi, Fiona! Hey, Amy. Cool bag! So many pockets."

Fiona's eyes were like shards of ice as Jenelle smiled back at Anderson. Fiona looked ready to strangle someone.

"Thanks, Anderson," I said. Anderson is my lab partner, and I can honestly say he's one of the sweetest people I've ever met. He's cute, too, with pale blond hair and pink cheeks. He and Jenelle are really adorable together, even though she's about two inches taller than him.

"Well, have fun," Fiona said, tossing her long black hair. "Whatever it is you're doing. Not that Jenelle ever tells me anything."

"Oh, I think we're going to —" But Anderson didn't get a chance to finish. Fiona had already stalked off. "I guess she was in a hurry," he said, half to himself.

"It's okay," Jenelle told him, but she didn't sound sure.

I knew what Jenelle meant. An angry Fiona was a dangerous thing to have around.

"Did you see that pink dress in the window at Veronique?" I asked my friends as I laced up my ice skates. We'd just spent the afternoon window-shopping at the Houston Galleria, and Mitchie had talked us into spending an hour on the ice. I'd never been to the indoor rink before, but I'd always wanted to try it. You could look down on the skaters from three levels of shops, and they always seemed to be having a great time, gliding around like floating birds.

"That dress was gorgeous," Mitchie said. "But not exactly the kind of thing you wear to school."

"Or on the half-pipe," Kiwi added.

Mitchie elbowed her in the ribs.

"I wonder if I could make it," I mused aloud. Sewing is kind of my hobby. I got into it because I really love fashion, but it's also a good skill to have because I'm usually kind of broke.

"Why would you need to make it?" Kiwi asked. "I'm pretty sure we've got one at Divine."

"Seriously?" I asked. Divine was Kiwi's parents' store. It was a thrift — I mean *resale* — shop, and all of the wealthiest ladies in Houston brought their clothes there once the season was over.

"What we have is really similar. But it's not pink — it's pale gray. And it might be a little too big for you," she added, frowning slightly.

"I could take it in," I told her. That would be a *lot* easier than starting from scratch. I finished tying my laces and tried to stand up. "Whoa!" I cried, windmilling my arms. Mitchie managed to catch me before I toppled over. "Does anyone else feel like their feet are encased in concrete?" I asked. Seriously, the skates felt like they weighed about five thousand pounds.

Mitchie laughed. "You'll get used to it."

I clung to the rail as Kiwi stepped out onto the ice. She was wearing a flowing Indian-print skirt over black leggings. The handkerchief-weight fabric fluttered as she floated onto the ice. She lifted her hands in the air and twisted them gracefully, like she was performing ballet.

Mitchie, on the other hand, barreled onto the ice like a race car. Glide, glide, then *whoosh* as she flipped a sudden turn and came to a dead stop. "Come on out," she urged, skating toward me with open arms.

I took a hesitant step onto the ice. "Yikes!" I cried as my foot slid away from me.

But Mitchie had grabbed both of my hands. "Just push out and away with each step, the way you would on in-line skates." She skated backward, still holding my hands as I wobbled onto the ice. Skaters zoomed past on either side of me. I felt like a turtle stuck in the center lane of the freeway — like I might get squashed at any second.

"This is way more slippery than in-line skates," I told her. I was really just kind of standing there, frozen.

"You've got it," Mitchie said encouragingly. "Now, just glide."

I slithered out with my right foot, then picked up my left. Suddenly, I was moving.

"That's it!" Mitchie said.

"Don't let go!" I shouted, but it was too late. She had released my hands, and I was sliding forward on my own.

"Don't think about it too much," Mitchie called as I flailed toward the rail at the edge of the rink. My fingers touched the edge — briefly — before I plopped down on my rear end.

"You've got to *feel* the ice," Kiwi sang as she fluttered past.

"I feel it," I said as she turned in a lazy, graceful circle nearby. "It feels *cold.* And wet," I added, swiping at my butt as I struggled to grab the railing. I hauled myself to my feet and tried to move forward. My feet slipped and slid beneath me as I inched along the wall. *How will I ever get back to the benches?* I wondered as I glanced over my shoulder. *Mitchie will have to haul me in, like a tugboat.*

"Hey, Flowers!" Anderson's voice floated overhead. Looking up, I saw him waving frantically at me through the Plexiglas barrier. Jenelle was with him.

"Don't just stand there!" I shouted. "I'm stuck — toss me a rope or something!"

They cracked up. "You're doing great, Amy!" Jenelle grinned. "It's your first time out, right?"

"No way — can't you tell I'm on the Olympic wall-clinging squad? I'm going for the gold!" They laughed, and I gestured toward the benches, trying to communicate that I wanted them to meet me over there. They seemed to get it, because they walked over to the entrance.

Somehow, I managed to slip and flail back to where I started. *Glonk, glonk, glonk.* I clomped over in my heavy skates and flopped onto a bench beside Jenelle. I was glad I had on dark denim jeans — the big wet spot on my backside wasn't as noticeable.

"Thank goodness that's over," I sighed. "I can't believe I made it back alive."

"You're really brave," Anderson said. "I've never had the guts to try ice-skating."

See what I mean? He really sees the best in everyone.

"What are you guys up to?" I asked.

"We just went to see *Agent X*," Jenelle said. "Over in Galleria II."

Um, yeah, that's right. The original Galleria — an enormous shopping mall — wasn't big enough, so they added Galleria II. Then they added Galleria III. It's like a humongous air-conditioned city of stuff to buy.

"How'd you like the movie?" I asked. It was a new action flick starring Nicole Pepper, one of my favorite actresses. "I've been dying to see it."

"It was amazing!" Anderson said, his blue eyes sparkling.

Just then, Mitchie skated up, sending a wave of shaved ice toward us as she sliced to a stop. I could have made a snow cone with the ice Mitchie was kicking up. "You okay, Amy?" she asked.

"Just taking a break," I told her.

"Hey, Mitchie," Anderson said. "You're as good on the ice as you are on a board."

Mitchie smiled shyly. "I used to take lessons," she explained. "My mom really wanted me to be an ice-skater, but it just wasn't me."

"I can't really see you in the glittery outfits," Jenelle put in. The minute the words were out of her mouth, I could tell that she wished she could take them back. I knew what she meant — short, sparkly skirts weren't exactly Mitchie's style. I didn't think that Jenelle meant it as an insult, but it kind of came out sounding that way.

And I could tell that was how Mitchie took it. She narrowed her eyes. "No, I guess that's not really my style," she said coldly.

"These guys just went to see *Agent X*," I broke in, eager to change the subject. "They say it's really good."

"Yeah, I wasn't sure I'd like it, but I did," Jenelle said, flashing me a grateful look.

Anderson grinned. "Lots of explosions."

Mitchie shrugged. "I saw it last weekend," she said.

"Did you love it?" Jenelle asked.

"Not really. I was kind of disappointed in Nicole Pepper's character. She was a complete marshmallow-brain and didn't get to do anything." Mitchie rolled her eyes as she leaned forward over the rails that separated us from the ice. "I *hate* movies where the guy gets to kick all of the butt, and the girl just sits beside him, giggling."

There was an awkward silence. Jenelle cast a sideways glance at me, and I sighed. Things had been pretty chilly between Mitchie and the League ever since Fiona pulled a mean prank on her last year. Fiona had invited Mitchie over for a slumber party, then cut off Mitchie's long hair while she was sleeping. Jenelle had been there, too, and she hadn't stopped it. Now, no matter what Jenelle did, Mitchie didn't seem to want to give her a chance. I mean, I understood her feelings. Still, it was kind of rough for me. I just wished my friends could get along.

"Well!" I said brightly. "I guess I'm going to try this skating deal one more time. You'll catch me if I fall, right, Mitchie?"

"Sure," she said as I clomped over to the edge.

"See you guys in school," I called, waving to Jenelle and Anderson.

"See you!" Anderson shouted. Jenelle just gave a little half-wave, like she was disappointed.

I don't blame her, I thought as I stepped back into the rink. Things between her and Mitchie were as cold as the ice under my feet, and twice as slippery. And I wasn't sure if they were ever going to thaw.

"Oh, ugh," I whispered to Mitchie as we stood in front of the huge, gleaming silver Allington buses lined up in front of the school. They rumbled quietly as Dean Denton read off a list of names in his sharp military voice. "Did they have to announce the assignments out here? I'm going to smell like Eau de Exhaust."

A smile curled at the corner of Mitchie's lips. "It's already five thousand degrees out here," she agreed. "I feel like a stick of butter in the microwave."

I knew what she meant. It was the first day of Step Out, and since we would be "representing Allington to the greater Houston community," the school had laid out a special dress code. Dresses or skirts for girls with — get this — panty hose or tights *required* (ugh!), and jackets and ties for boys. It was only March, but it was eighty-five degrees already. The humidity made me feel like I was coated in a fine film of grime, and the panty hose were making me feel like a sausage. Just imagine a dusty hot dog tossed on the grill, and you've pretty much got the effect.

"Volunteers for Belle Manor Rest Home," Mr. Denton barked, looking down at his clipboard. "Josie Banks, Emmett Daly, Brooke Rosen, Don Trebuchet . . ." The sun gleamed off his bald head. "Please board bus number one."

Emmett and Don high-fived and clambered onto the bus. Those guys were in my math class and were serious jokers. I wondered if the senior citizens at the rest home knew what they were in for.

Someone gave me a friendly poke in the side. "Think they'll be having wheelchair races in the hallways?" Jenelle whispered, nodding at Emmett and Don. Fiona and Lucia were standing to her right, staring straight ahead with stony faces.

I giggled, and Mitchie looked over. Her smile disappeared when she saw Jenelle and the rest of the League.

Mr. Denton flashed us a glare. "Montrose Botanical Association Tranquillity Garden," he read in a tone that warned, *Don't make me force you to stop whispering, girls.* "Cairdwyn Adair . . ."

"Yes," Mitchie hissed, pumping her fist. Cairdwyn was Kiwi's real name.

"George James III, Michiko Ohara, Brody Brooks, Jenelle Renwick, and Pear Waters."

"*Tranquillity* Garden?" Fiona snapped. She

looked Jenelle up and down, surveying her white eyelet dress. "Have fun digging in the dirt."

"Yeah, like, you're wearing a white outfit?" Lucia pointed out. "That was, like, not great planning?"

Mitchie turned to Jenelle, who was blushing.

Awkward silence pulsed between them.

Oh, boy, I thought. I scanned the ground for a rock to hide under.

"So . . . you're doing the community garden?" Jenelle asked finally.

"Obviously," Mitchie said. "I guess we both are."

And the silence stretched on. . . .

"Omigoshomigoshomigosh!" Kiwi squealed as she hurried over. She flung her arms around Mitchie and Jenelle, squeezing them together. "This is going to be *so* great!"

That's what I love about Kiwi — she's pretty oblivious to tension. For her, life is just a bucket of sunshine and unicorns.

"Ms. Adair, if you've finished disturbing everyone else, would you kindly board bus number three?" Mr. Denton was glowering our way, his bald head gleaming menacingly.

"Sure thing, sir!" Kiwi singsonged. She grabbed Jenelle's right hand and Mitchie's left, and dragged them toward the buses.

"Poor Jenelle," Fiona sighed.

I ignored her as the dean read off more assignments. One by one and in small groups, kids headed off toward their buses. Finally, he read, "Health on the Move Experience. The volunteers are Amy Flowers, Preston Harringford, and Fiona Von Steig."

"What?" Lucia shrieked. Everyone turned to look at her. She didn't notice though, because she was too busy gaping at Fiona, who was staring straight ahead with a strange little smile on her face. "I thought the Health-car-thingie was ridiculous?" Lucia hissed. "I thought we were volunteering in the soup kitchen?"

"I said that *you* should volunteer in the soup kitchen," Fiona corrected. "I never said *I* would."

"But I thought —" Lucia looked hurt. "I thought —"

"I don't force you to listen to me, do I?" Fiona snapped, and she turned sharply and headed toward bus three.

Lucia stood there blinking back tears as Mr. Denton read off the names for the soup kitchen. At that moment, I wished I were friendly enough with Lucia to give her a hug. She looked like she needed it. But I didn't think a hug from me would really make her feel much better. Instead,

I flashed her a sympathetic look as I made my way to the bus. She just frowned at me and turned away, skimming her bottom eyelashes with an index finger, like she was wiping away tears.

Oh, well. I sighed.

Air-conditioning washed over me like cool water as I stepped onto bus three.

"Yay!" Kiwi cried when she saw me. She pointed to the empty seat across from where she and Mitchie were sitting. "I was hoping you'd get this bus!"

"Did you get the Healthmobile?" Mitchie asked.

"Yep," I said as I flopped into the seat. "And you'll never guess who else did, too."

"Oh, I'll bet I can," Mitchie said drily. She jutted her chin at a seat two rows ahead of hers, where a certain black-haired beauty sat stiff-backed, staring straight ahead. "Does her name rhyme with Shmee-ohn-wah?"

I nodded. "Yep. And the other person's name rhymes with —"

"Intestines," Preston said as he plopped down in the seat next to mine.

"What?" I blinked at him. I mean, "Preston" and "intestines" did kind of rhyme, but . . .

"I said, 'I hope we don't have to work with the intestines,'" Preston repeated. "I hear that section is kind of gross."

"What are you talking about?" I asked him. I looked over at Mitchie, who shrugged in confusion.

"The health units are broken into parts of the body," he explained. "The first section is muscle, then stomach, then lung — that's the antismoking part — then intestines."

"The whole thing sounds pretty disgusting," Mitchie said.

"That's why the little kids love it." Preston waggled his eyebrows. "You've got to know your audience. Personally, I think the section they need to do is —"

"Don't say it." I held up my hand.

Preston grinned. "Don't say what?" He winked at Kiwi, who giggled.

"Whatever it was that you were going to say," I told him. "Because I'm sure it's something way grosser than 'intestines.'"

"I was going to say 'brain,'" Preston said in a haughty voice. "Jeez. I'd think a *genius* like you would love to have a brain section."

I gritted my teeth. Preston is always teasing me because I'm a good student. I mean, whatever —

he's as smart as I am. We were even on the Academic Challenge team together. It's not my fault if his grades don't show it.

Preston dug in his backpack and pulled out a lollipop. "Want one?" he asked.

"No, thanks."

"Are you sure?" he singsonged playfully. "This is the last sugar you'll get until we all escape from Healthville at three fifteen." He dangled it in front of my face and I batted it away lightly.

"No, thank you," I repeated.

"Suit yourself," he said. "But you'll regret it. What about you guys?" he asked, turning to Kiwi and Mitchie.

"What flavor?" Kiwi asked.

I rolled my eyes. I couldn't believe Kiwi was falling for Preston's nice routine. *Doesn't she know he's just trying to find a way to drive me crazy?* I wondered as Preston dug around in his bag again and produced a rainbow of lollipops. "I've got grape, strawberry, watermelon, lemon, and kiwi," he said.

"You've got kiwi flavor?" Kiwi asked eagerly. Her brown eyes were huge. "Really?"

"Actually, I think it's lime," Preston admitted. "But it's green."

Kiwi laughed. "I'll take strawberry."

Preston handed it over. "Excellent choice."

"I'll take grape," Mitchie said as Kiwi ripped the cellophane off of her candy.

"Ah — I dig people who respect the classic flavors." Preston nodded his approval as he passed Mitchie the purple lollipop. He stood up, smoothing his red-striped tie with long fingers. "Looks like we're coming to the first stop. I'd better go talk Emmett and Don out of their plans to steal a gurney and fifteen rolls of gauze before we get to Belle Manor." He headed down the aisle as the bus hissed to a standstill at the curb.

"This lollipop is *so* good," Kiwi gushed. "And I don't usually even like lollipops!"

"I wonder where Preston got them," Mitchie said. "My grape really tastes like grape — not like the fake grape you usually get." The sweet, heavy scent of fruit floated past my nose, making my mouth water. I had to admit, those lollipops did smell good.

"You should have taken one, Amy," Kiwi said. "Preston is so great!"

"Sometimes."

"Oh, come on. He's always nice!" Kiwi insisted.

"Except when he's annoying," I said. "Which is usually."

"I think he's funny," Mitchie put in. "What?" she asked when I shot her a look.

I sighed. Now I had to spend every afternoon for the next two weeks with Fiona and Preston . . . and it didn't even look like I was going to get an ounce of sympathy for it.

I should have taken the lollipop.

CHAPTER THREE

Health Hint:
No two people smell the same odor the same way. (For example, some people may find pine-scented cleaner to smell vaguely like toxic waste.)

Preston was right about the intestines.

"Are these people serious?" Fiona muttered as we stepped into the Health on the Move Experience trailer. The outside of the trailer was marked HOME in big red letters; inside, it was filled with displays and equipment. "What a dump."

"Check it out!" Preston said as he flipped a switch. A human skeleton sprang to life. It was wearing a top hat and did a little jig. "This place is seriously weird! I love it!"

I stepped farther into the HOME. It wasn't *really* a dump . . . although it did look as if about fifteen thousand kids had run through it after playing soccer in a mud factory. And I did have to agree with Preston — it was kind of weird. It was a large trailer divided into sections. The first part had all of the stuff about food and nutrition. The lung section had a large display made of something pink and spongy, and a television monitor set into the center that showed a film about the dangers of smoking. The display for "Digestion Central" was ridged and slippery . . . like intestines, I supposed. And the rear section had everything you'd need to teach about exercise. Take a bow, Mr. Dancing Skeleton.

"Oh, great," Anthony said as he appeared in the doorway. "You're here. I'm Anthony Porter." He was wearing a canary-yellow polo shirt that showed off his dark-brown skin. *Anthony Porter is even better-looking up close,* I noticed. I hadn't even realized that it was *possible* to be better-looking than he was before.

"Fiona Von Steig." Fiona held out her fingers, almost as if she expected Anthony to kiss her hand or something. Like she was the Queen of England.

He shook her hand awkwardly. "Um, nice to meet you. And I see you brought two assistants."

Fiona tossed back her head and laughed, as if that was the funniest thing she'd ever heard anyone say.

Preston cocked an eyebrow at her. "Yeah, I'm Preston, and this is Amy."

"Welcome aboard the HOME," Anthony said, flashing me a smile. "I see Allington slapped you guys with the dress code. They don't bother telling us juniors what to wear."

I waited for him to say, "Don't worry about it after today," but he didn't.

"Oh, I usually wear a skirt, anyway," Fiona piped up. "Unlike some people, I think it's important to look nice." She smirked at me.

Just then, a woman with close-cropped hair stepped into the HOME. She had warm brown eyes and was wearing a tailored pantsuit with a colorful scarf. "Welcome, everyone! I'm Ms. Greene, and I'm officially in charge of the Health on the Move Experience project." She put the word "officially" in finger quotes.

"But I'll handle most of the day-to-day stuff," Anthony said quickly.

Ms. Greene checked her watch. "Tony, would you mind filling everyone in and getting the day started? I've got to meet with the principal in seven minutes."

"Absolutely," he said.

"So . . ." Fiona said brightly once Ms. Greene had left. "Do you want to give us a tour of the trailer, Tony?"

Anthony cocked his head and looked at her coldly. "Don't call me Tony," he said.

"Oh, I — sorry —" Fiona turned a shade of red that I usually associate with ketchup.

I had to bite my lip to keep from giggling.

Anthony showed us around the trailer, explaining how everything worked. It was a pretty long, detailed tour — especially considering that the entire trailer was only about thirty feet long. It took an hour at least. Finally, at the end of the lecture, he stopped at a small closet. "And this is where the fun really begins for you guys," he said. "This is a special space just for volunteers."

"Yeah?" Preston asked eagerly. "Great! What's inside?"

Anthony opened the door to reveal a set of brooms and mops, sponges and dusters, and a yellow bucket on wheels. The bucket was filled with water that reeked of fake pine scent. "Your first job."

"Oh, ew!" Fiona flapped her manicured fingers in front of her nose. "I'm not touching that stuff."

"Hey, hey, hey!" Anthony snapped his fingers in her face. *Snap! Snap! Snap!* "Let's have a little more of the Allington spirit!" He handed her a pair of rubber gloves. "Health is important, my friends, and you can't teach people about health if your displays are crawling with germs, can you?"

Fiona's jaw dropped, and her face turned a very interesting shade of magenta. She looked furious, and I didn't blame her. Anthony was seeming less and less dreamy with each passing second. She opened her mouth to say something, but Preston cut her off.

"Sounds great, Anthony," he said, snatching the yellow rubber gloves. He started rolling up his sleeves. "I'm sure you've got important health stuff to do, so we'll just get to work in here." He pulled on the gloves.

This seemed to chill Anthony out a little. "Yeah, I do have some stuff to do," he admitted. "The school is letting us use one of their small offices, so that's where I'll be if you need me. And, hey, don't worry. You won't have to clean the HOME every day. It's just that tomorrow is our first day with the kids, and we want everything to look good."

Preston saluted. "We'll have this stuff shipshape in no time."

Anthony looked over at me uncertainly, as if he suspected that Preston might be making fun of him. Honestly, I kind of suspected the same thing. But it didn't seem worth it to make Anthony angry. So I just said, "We're on it," and smiled.

"*You're* on it," Fiona muttered under her breath. "I'm *over* it."

But nobody heard her except me.

"Okay." Anthony hovered in the doorway for another moment, then finally turned and left.

Preston let out a long breath. "Now, that is someone who takes being in Healthville very seriously."

"Well, just think about tomorrow," I told him. "It'll be fun once we're actually working with the kids." I grabbed a mop and pulled the bucket out of the closet.

"Here you go," Preston said, handing Fiona a broom.

Her eyebrows arched nearly to her hairline. "You're kidding, right?"

"Would you rather scrub the displays?" Preston asked.

"I'd *rather* get out of this insane trailer," Fiona snapped. She folded her arms across her chest and sat down on an enormous model of the human heart. "And never come back."

"No way," I said, tossing a rag in her direction. It landed on something that looked vaguely like a giant green bean. *What is that?* I wondered. *A spleen?* "You're not sticking Preston and me with all of the work. Go dust something."

Fiona snorted. "Fine." She picked up the rag between her thumb and forefinger, and halfheartedly began to dust the bean.

Preston flashed me a little smile, like he was impressed that I'd managed to get Fiona to do something. I felt myself blush slightly. I don't even know why. Looking down quickly, I yanked on my mop, which was stuck in the bucket's wringer. I tried to pull it out, but it wouldn't budge. And when I fiddled with the lever on the side, I only seemed to make things worse.

"Mind if I try?" Preston asked.

I backed away from the bucket. "Go for it."

He gave the lever a hard yank, but nothing happened. "Hm." His finger hooked into the wringer as he tried to fish something out. "Something's stuck in there," he said, leaning over the bucket. "I think I got it!" he said, pulling out a long, twisted mop strand.

"Great news!" I said. "But . . . uh . . . there's some bad news, too." I pointed to his tie.

Preston looked confused, then glanced down. His tie was dangling in the dirty mop water. I expected him to get mad or at least let out a groan, but instead, Preston threw back his head and laughed.

"I think I'm going to be sick," Fiona said from her place by the food pyramid display. "That water smells like a combination of fake pine and toxic waste."

"Sorry," I said. I felt bad. He'd ruined his tie helping me.

"Eh, I hate this tie anyway," Preston said, yanking at the knot by his neck. "Now I have an excuse to take it off."

"And an excuse to burn it," Fiona added.

Preston tossed his tie in the corner beside his backpack, and we all got to work. We dusted all of the displays, wiped down the touch screens, swept, mopped, scrubbed the baseboards, organized pamphlets, sharpened pencils, cleaned out the supply closet, took out the trash, and generally got everything in order for the next day.

"I think that's it," Preston said finally. He'd just taken out the bucket and emptied the dirty water.

I looked around. The place was immaculate. "Great job!" I said, giving Preston a high five.

"My arms hurt," Fiona griped. She was back in her seat on the heart. "Cleaning is exhausting."

"Yeah, dusting is a real physical challenge," Preston teased.

At that moment, Anthony reappeared in the doorway. I smiled proudly as he stepped inside and surveyed our job. Some of the grime we'd scrubbed out looked pretty ancient. I was almost sure that the HOME hadn't looked this good in years.

"This seems fine," Anthony said finally. "But you missed a spot." He pointed to a tiny black mark on the wall near the floor. It was half hidden by the heart.

Are you kidding me? I wanted to ask, but Preston just leaned over quietly and scrubbed it with a rag.

"That's better." Anthony nodded. "I guess you guys can go now. The bus will be here to pick you up in a few minutes." He turned to walk away.

My stomach let out a low rumble, and that was when I realized that Anthony hadn't given us a lunch break. I always get my lunch at the Allington cafeteria. The chefs there are some of the best in Houston, and — since I'm on a scholarship — I get to eat for free. I guess I'd expected that we would be able to buy a lunch at McClure, but Anthony didn't show us where to go or say it was okay. Suddenly, I was completely starving.

"Hey, is the cafeteria still open?" Preston asked, as if he had read my mind. "Maybe we can grab something to eat."

"It's closed now," Anthony called over his shoulder. "There's a diner up the street." He didn't break his stride as he walked toward the school.

"I'm there," Preston said. He looked at Fiona. "Who's in? We'll just call our parents and let them know to pick us up later, and they can call the school."

"Forget it," Fiona said. "I'm going home. I can't live with this disinfectant smell in my hair for an extra five seconds."

Preston turned to me. I was tempted to say no. I wanted to wash the grime off, too, and besides I was dog tired. On the other hand, I was so hungry that I could actually visualize gnawing on my purse's leather strap. "I'll come," I said. "If I can use your cell phone to call my dad." He worked nearby, and I knew it would be no problem for him to pick me up later.

"Really?" Preston looked surprised. For a moment, I thought he might say something more. Then he seemed to decide against it. "Okay," he said, handing over his cell phone.

"Why not?" I started to punch in my dad's work number. "We need to talk about what we're going to do for our final project, anyway."

"You two are crazy," Fiona said. "I don't need to talk about the final project because I'm going to make sure Allington gives me a different assignment."

I rolled my eyes. *Good*, I thought.

But I suspected that I'd never get that lucky.

"Um . . ." I paged through the menu as the waitress stood there looking bored. She was tall and thin, and was dressed as if she'd probably worked in this same diner for thirty years. "I think I'll have a burger — no, wait —" I turned another page. This was one seriously hefty menu. "A club sandwich. That's it. No, wait —"

Preston groaned. "Come on," he complained. "Some of us are starving."

"I'll have the spicy chicken wrap." I closed the menu and shoved it away so I wouldn't be tempted by anything else.

The waitress pursed her lips, her pencil hovering over her pad. "Fries?"

I shook my head, but Preston said yes. "And I'll have a roast beef sandwich on wheat and a banana split with double the hot fudge sauce and peanut

M&M'S on top. But please bring the banana split out first, okay?"

The waitress just nodded. "Whipped cream? Nuts? Cherry?"

"Everything but the nuts," Preston told her, handing back the menu.

"You eat dessert first?" I asked him.

"Whenever I can get away with it."

I smiled. "But what if you aren't hungry for the sandwich afterward?"

"Don't worry, I will be. But even if I wasn't, it's a bigger risk to eat the sandwich first. Then I might not be hungry for the banana split!"

"Um, exactly," I told him.

"I'm glad you agree." Preston blew the wrapper off of his straw and took a sip of his lemonade.

I shook my head. "Didn't you read all of the information on the Healthmobile?" I teased. "You're flying in the face of basic nutrition!"

"I didn't have time to read that stuff — I was too busy scrubbing off the gunk that had collected behind the giant model of the human spleen. Besides, if Anthony was so interested in our health, he would have let us eat lunch."

I had to admit that he had a point. It seemed like a pretty tempting point, too, as the waitress set the banana split down in front of him.

"I bet you're sorry now." Preston dug his spoon through a cloud of whipped cream. "Mmmmmmmmmm!"

I laughed and took a bite of my chicken wrap. "This is good, too," I told him. "And it won't rot my teeth." I tried to sound perfectly satisfied with my sandwich, but it was hard when that ice cream looked so good.

"Check this out," Preston said, plucking a yellow M&M from the top of a mountain of whipped cream. He leaned his head back and spat the M&M into the air. It hung there a moment, then dropped right back into his open mouth.

Preston grinned at me, and held up his hands in a little "ta-da!" gesture.

"That is disgusting," I said.

He chewed the candy a moment, pretending to think it over. "True," he admitted. "But you're secretly impressed."

"Oh, that definitely made an impression," I told him, laughing.

"So, what do you think of the Healthmobile?" he asked, digging into a pool of hot fudge.

"It's cool," I told him. "There's a lot of good information there, and the displays are fun." I took a bite of my sandwich. It was delicious. Not banana-split delicious, of course, but you can't exactly throw M&M'S in with spicy chicken.

"But what did you think of the exercise section?" he asked. "I mean, doesn't it seem weird that we would stand around, *talking* to kids about exercise?"

"So, you think we should get them to move around? Actually do a little exercise?"

"Why not?" Preston demanded. "It just seems like you don't really have to tell kids to like exercise. They always do — as long as they don't know it's exercise. If you tell them it's a sport or a game, they're into it."

I nodded, and Preston went on. "I think we should try to come up with some stuff we can do in that small space. I know when I was that age, I had a lot of trouble sitting still, anyway."

"Shocking," I joked.

Preston just smiled. "So, what do you think?"

"I think it sounds like a great idea," I told him honestly. "Maybe we'll even get extra credit on our final project."

"I like the way you think, Amy Flowers." Preston tapped his temple and gave me a goofy wink, which made me crack up. *I'm actually having fun with Preston Harringford*, I realized.

“Amy?” said a familiar voice. I looked up into a pair of chocolate-brown eyes, and my stomach gave a lurch.

I tried to say, “Hey, Scott,” in a totally casual voice, but it came out sounding squeaky and weird. I cleared my throat and pointed to my neck, in an attempt to make it seem as if the spicy chicken had affected my powers of speech.

Scott nodded at Preston. “Hey, what’s up? I didn’t expect to see you two here.” He looked from Preston to me, then back again. I wasn’t sure, but I thought I caught a slight emphasis on the words “you two.”

“We just finished our volunteering,” I explained quickly.

“Yeah, the guy in charge didn’t give us a lunch break,” Preston added. “He’s a real charmer.”

Scott laughed politely. He and Preston were both on the soccer team, so they knew each other. Also, all of us had been on the same Academic Challenge team, along with Mitchie. I couldn’t figure out why it felt so freaky to be talking to both of them now. All I knew was that I wanted one of us to leave — Scott, Preston, or me — and I didn’t really care which.

I guess Scott felt uncomfortable, too. “So, uh, I’ll see you this weekend?” he asked.

"I'll be there," I promised.

"Cool." He nodded, then turned to Preston. "See you later, man." Then he walked off toward a corner table, where a bunch of other eighth-grade Allington guys were sitting.

Preston looked down at his banana split and took a slow, careful spoonful. But he didn't eat it. Instead, he asked, "So, what's this weekend?"

"Some fancy party," I told him. I squirmed in my seat. Suddenly, this vinyl booth seemed incredibly uncomfortable.

Preston nodded, then took another bite of his banana split. "Cool. Scott's a great guy."

"Yeah," I said.

We looked at each other a moment, and I felt my heart pulsing through my neck. I don't know why I felt so embarrassed that Preston knew about my semi-date with Scott. *What is there to be embarrassed about?* I asked myself.

I couldn't come up with an answer.

"So, about the Healthmobile," Preston said quickly. And he went on to lay out a few of his ideas. But I could hardly concentrate. I just sat there, nodding and eating my chicken wrap, my brain jumbled with thoughts about Preston and Scott.

CHAPTER FOUR

**Health Hint:
Elephants can cry.
So can sea otters, seals,
and crocodiles.
Oh, and humans.**

"How can I have a closet stuffed with clothes and nothing to wear?" I griped as I flipped through hanger after hanger.

It was Wednesday afternoon, and Mitchie was sprawled on my bed, leafing through a magazine with one hand and petting Pizza, my little white dog, with another. "Because *nobody* has anything to wear to a wedding shower," she said. "I don't even know what you're *supposed* to wear."

"I don't know, either — a decent skirt and a nice top, I guess." I bit my lip and frowned at a black skirt. *Too dark,* I thought. *But maybe I could wear it with a pink shirt. If I* had *a pink shirt . . .*

"Really? I was thinking hoop skirt and bonnet." Pizza nuzzled Mitchie's hand, eager to be scratched behind the ears. "Oh, that's perfect!" she said, nodding at a skirt I'd just pulled out. It had a large orange-and-green flower print.

I gave her a dubious look. "This skirt makes me look like a sofa."

"Right," Mitchie agreed. "Isn't that the kind of thing people wear to a shower?"

The hanger hit the rod with a *click* as I put the skirt back in the closet. "You call this helping?" I asked her. "Linda's shower is in two hours!" I still had to shower, dry my hair, and get dressed before Jenelle's mother's party. And I couldn't help wondering if I'd made a mistake when I invited Mitchie to come over and help me pick out something to wear. After all, she doesn't even like Jenelle. Why would she care if I wore something ugly to Jenelle's mother's bridal shower?

With a groan, Mitchie hauled herself off my bed and stood next to me. She reached into the closet and pulled out an oversized shirt with huge polka dots and stripes at the collar. "You actually spent money on this?" she asked.

"I made it," I told her.

"Oh." She winced and put the shirt back in the closet. "Sorry. It's . . . um . . . really different."

"It was my Halloween costume two years ago," I explained. "I went as a clown."

Mitchie breathed a sigh of relief. "Oh, good." She flipped through a few hangers and finally pulled out a khaki dress. "This," she said.

"Ha-ha."

Mitchie shook her head. "No, I'm serious."

"Really?" I glanced at the dress. My aunt Rita had given it to me as a Christmas present a year ago. I'd never known what to do with it. "Isn't it a little 'jungle safari'? What do I wear it with — a pith helmet?"

"Don't you have a pair of gold hoop earrings?" Mitchie asked.

"Sure."

"Okay, wear those. Then go with your red wedge shoes and your watch with the wide red strap. It'll look great."

I could actually picture the outfit in my mind. It kind of seemed like it might work. "Wow," I said. I'd asked Mitchie to help me because I knew she'd be honest if something was truly hideous. I hadn't really expected her to be able to pull together a whole outfit like that.

"I'll do your hair," Mitchie promised. "How about this?" She picked up the magazine and pointed to a photo. The girl's hair was swept back in a low-on-the-neck updo. A few romantic tendrils hung around her face.

"Seriously?" I asked. "You think you can do it?"

Mitchie studied my hair, then nodded. "I can make it work," she promised.

"Knock, knock," Kirk said as he barged into my room.

"Why don't you just *actually* knock?" I asked him.

"Because I live to annoy you," he said. Kirk smiled at Mitchie. "I *thought* I heard your voice. What are you doing here?"

Mitchie beamed. "Just helping Amy pick out something to wear to a bridal shower."

"Hey, how about that clown costume from two years ago?" Kirk suggested.

"That was the first thing I picked out," Mitchie said with a laugh.

"What do you do at a bridal shower, anyway?" Kirk asked, moving to pet Pizza, who had rolled onto her back in the hope of a belly rub. "Drink tea?"

"Talk in a fake British accent?" Mitchie joined in.

"Ew, loooovely weather we're having, isn't it?" Kirk asked in the world's worst English accent. "Isn't it just divine that our dear Linda has found a beau at last?" Then he pretended to take a huge slurp of tea.

"Don't you have somewhere else to be right now?" I asked him. "Like, *anywhere* else?"

"Actually, I was heading down to the driveway to practice a few tricks on my board." He turned to Mitchie. "Want to join?"

Mitchie's eyes widened, and she glanced at me with an "Ohpleaseohpleaseohplease" look. But what she said was, "Well, I promised I'd help Amy."

It took me a minute to process what was happening. Clearly, my friend was crushing. Hard. But did Kirk feel the same way? I had no idea. Part of me felt like I'd be doing Mitchie a favor by asking her to stay with me. After all, Kirk was in high school. I didn't think it was too likely that he'd be into one of my friends. Why should she get her hopes up?

Then again, judging by the flush in her cheeks and the sparkle in her black eyes, it looked like they were already up. Way up.

"You've already helped me pick out an outfit," I said finally. "I need to shower and stuff. Why don't you come back in a little while and help me with my hair?"

"Sounds great!" Mitchie said quickly.

"Cool." Kirk grinned, and the two of them took

off to invade our driveway. I looked out my window and watched them spill out the door, each carrying a board. Mitchie showed Kirk a few tricks, and Kirk copied them. Well, he copied them in the way that a kindergartner copies the alphabet — backward and all over the place. But he didn't seem to mind it when Mitchie corrected him. My friend was so much better on her board, it was actually kind of ridiculous. But I had to give Kirk props. He kept on trying and didn't give up. Even though he kept falling on his butt, looking like a fool. Usually, Kirk hates looking like an idiot in front of anyone. A couple of weeks ago, I offered to help him with a set of math problems that were stumping him. He just called me "Brainiac" and stormed out of the room.

I wondered why it was different with Mitchie.

Glancing at the clock, I realized that I had to get a move on or I'd be late. I hurried to the bathroom and did my usual extra-short shower. Then I hopped out and got dressed as quickly as I could. Kirk and Mitchie walked in just as I was tugging on my shoes.

"I think you're getting it," Mitchie was saying.

Kirk laughed. "If by 'it' you mean 'bruises,' then I think you're right."

Just then, the phone rang. The cordless was

lying on the table in the hall, so I grabbed it. "Hello?"

"Hi," said a smooth, feminine voice. "May I please speak to Kirk?"

"Um, sure," I said. I held out the phone to my brother. "It's for you."

"Oh, it's probably the X Games," Kirk joked as he took the receiver. "Hello? Oh, hi." His voice turned suddenly serious. "Uh . . . it's . . . uh . . . it's great to hear from you. Listen, uh, just hold on a minute." He turned to Mitchie. "Hey, thanks for the lesson. I'll see you around, okay?" And he hustled to his room and shut the door.

Mitchie turned to me. She was beaming, and her cheeks were pink from the exercise. She looked beautiful. "Are you ready for your hairstyle?" she asked. She didn't seem to notice the change in Kirk.

"Sure," I said. We walked toward my room, but I couldn't help glancing down the hall. I could hear Kirk's voice, but I couldn't make out the words.

Who is that girl on the phone? I wondered. I guessed I could ask Kirk later . . . but I wasn't sure I wanted to know.

"Would you care for anozer mini crepe?" The elegant waitress held out a silver platter heaped with tiny fruit-filled French pancake things. They were *so* good. I'd already had about ten of them.

I'm sure she hasn't noticed, I told myself as I took two more and placed them on my plate. "Thanks."

The waitress winked at me. "I'll be back in anozer ten minutes," she said in her French accent, which made me giggle.

I guess she noticed.

"Isn't this beautiful?" my mom asked as she touched one of the tendrils around my face.

"It's the most amazing party I've ever seen," I said warmly. Linda had rented a room in a small, elegant French restaurant in the Rice Village. The bridal shower's theme was "April in Paris," which meant that the place was bursting with enormous, colorful flower arrangements. The polite waitstaff floated around the room offering food and drinks, but you could also help yourself at the buffet table lined with platters of quiche and croissant sandwiches. There was even a five-foot-tall Eiffel Tower made of chocolate at the center. "It's way better than I expected."

"Actually, I meant that I thought your *hair* was beautiful," Mom said with a smile. "Mitchie did a wonderful job. But you're right — Linda has great taste."

"What's that? Did I hear my name?" Linda fluttered over toward us, a wide smile spread across her face. She was absolutely glowing. "I'm *so* glad you two are here — I hope you're having a good time. Did you try one of the crepes yet, Amy? They're scrumptious! Jean Pierre is a miracle worker, I'm telling you."

I couldn't help laughing. "I had a crepe."

"Where did Jenelle go?" Linda asked.

"I don't know," I said, looking around the room. I didn't see anyone my age — just a mix of well-groomed and artistic ladies, Linda's friends and close family. "She and Fiona both disappeared a while ago."

"Would you go find them, sweetheart? We're about to start opening presents." Linda rolled her eyes a little. "I always feel like such a fool with everyone sitting around watching me as I unwrap things. But that's what you do at a shower, I guess!"

"I'll find Jenelle," I promised, just as a woman in a fitted red dress began clapping her hands and announcing that it was time for presents.

I ducked into the ladies' room, but it was empty except for a dignified woman in a black outfit. She was sitting on a stool, and it took me a long time to realize that she was the attendant. She looked like she should be hosting *Best American Model. What is with this restaurant?* I wondered. They seemed to hire only gorgeous people.

"Oh, isn't this delightful!" Linda was exclaiming as I stepped out of the bathroom. "A spa weekend for two at Lotus Ranch! Louise, how generous — thank you!"

The women who were clustered around let out an appreciative "ooooh" as Linda held up the Lotus Ranch brochure. Mom was sitting at the edge of the group, and I caught her eye as Linda tore the paper off of the next gift. It was enormous, and when the paper peeled back, I saw that Linda's sister had given her a giant high-definition television. "Lovely!" Linda exclaimed. "Steve will adore it!"

My mother looked from me toward the gift we had placed on the table along with the others. The pink-and-purple-striped package was the only one that looked as if it hadn't been wrapped by a professional. I wondered if Mom was thinking the same thing I was — that our gift seemed pretty meager compared to the others. We'd found an old photo of Uncle Steve in a box of Dad's college stuff, and Mom had had it framed. The frame was silver and very pretty, but I was starting to think that maybe we should have gotten one made of gold and encrusted with diamonds if we wanted to hang out in this crowd.

I was actually grateful that I had an excuse to escape. I felt the heat rise in my cheeks as I darted toward the back door, which opened on to a garden patio. Just as I stepped toward the door, Fiona came barreling through. She wasn't watching where she was going, and I didn't have time to leap out of the way, so she slammed into my shoulder. When she looked up at me in surprise, I saw that there were tears in her eyes.

"Are you okay?" I asked.

Instantly, her expression hardened. "Wouldn't *you* like to know?" she snapped, and stalked off.

I watched her for a moment, then turned back toward the patio. Stepping out into the evening moonlight, I saw that Jenelle was sitting on a bench, staring down at her cell phone. She looked Grade-A miserable. Clearly, I'd just walked in on a fight. After Fiona's reaction, I wasn't sure if I should ask Jenelle if she was all right, or just tiptoe away. I'd almost decided to go with the tiptoe when Jenelle looked up. "Oh, Amy," she said. Her smile was wobbly, but it worked. "Hi."

"Is everything —"

Jenelle shook her head, and I sat down beside her.

"Do you want to talk about it?" I asked.

Jenelle heaved a sigh. "It's kind of a long story."

"I don't really have to be anywhere," I told her. "Until they kick us out of the restaurant."

Jenelle gave me the kind of look that you give when you know someone is trying to make you feel better, but it isn't really working. "Well, Anderson called this morning. He sounded really hurt, and he wanted to know why I stood him up for our date yesterday after school."

"Did something come up?" I asked.

"No. We didn't have a date. At least — not that I knew of. But Anderson said that he'd gotten my text telling him to meet me at Cue Café. He'd waited there for three hours before finally running into friends who could give him a ride home. He'd left his phone in his dad's car, so he couldn't even call me."

I shook my head. "I'm missing something — what does this have to do with Fiona?"

"How many people could send someone a text from my phone without me knowing about it?" Jenelle's hazel gaze was calm, but I could see rage there, too.

"Just one," I admitted.

Jenelle pressed her lips together. "You know," she said after a moment, "I always thought that Fiona and I were true friends. I thought she'd never turn against me."

I didn't know what to say, so I just nodded. Of course, I knew someone else who had thought the same thing.

"I know she doesn't want me to go out with Anderson — but what business is it of hers?" Jenelle demanded.

"Seriously," I agreed. I really didn't understand why Fiona cared so much.

"Anyway, I told her that . . . that I don't want to be friends anymore," Jenelle said. There was just the slightest hesitation in her voice.

"What else were you supposed to do?" I asked.

"I don't know."

We were silent. The patio was lined with potted cypress trees and tall purple flowers that smelled wonderful. I would have pointed out how pretty everything was . . . but Jenelle seemed too miserable to enjoy it.

"Let's go inside," Jenelle said finally. "Mom is probably looking for me."

"She sent me to find you," I admitted.

Jenelle nodded. "I hope I didn't miss all of the presents."

I took her hand and led her inside, where Linda was holding up a familiar-looking package wrapped in pink and purple stripes. "This one is from Amy and Diane Flowers," she said as she tore off the paper. I winced a little as Linda sat there, looking at our gift in surprise. "Oh," she said.

I felt a blush working its way up from my toes.

It was all I could do not to leap forward and say, "Ha-ha! That's just a joke! Our *real* gift is something else — something way better!" But I didn't. I just stood there, while Linda's fingers pressed against her lips.

The whole room was quiet. I saw my mother shifting in her chair as if someone had put a tack beneath her.

"I'm sorry," Linda said after a moment. "This is just —" She blinked hard, trying to clear the tears that had collected in her eyes. "This is just the most beautiful present that anyone has ever given me." Her voice was thick with emotion as she turned the photo for everyone to see. There was Uncle Steve, in his college days. He'd been the emcee of a special comedy night, and he was wearing a tux and his trademark goofy grin. He was holding out a top hat, as if beckoning the viewer to join him for a dance.

"Aww . . ." chorused the ladies in the room.

“Thank you so much, Amy and Diane,” Linda said, beaming through her tears. “This is just lovely. I’m —” Her voice broke a little. “I’m so glad we’re family.” My mother hurried over to give her a hug.

Jenelle nudged me in the ribs. “Nice work . . . *cousin*,” she whispered as our mothers embraced.

I felt myself blushing again. Only this time, it was from happiness.

CHAPTER FIVE

Health Hint:
Every day, about 3,000 teens start smoking. About a third of those will eventually die of smoking-related diseases. (So snuff it out!)

"And who can tell me where I would find bulgur on the food pyramid?" Anthony asked as he stood at the front of the first-grade class. He motioned to the large food pyramid poster behind him. "Where would bulgur be?"

The class was silent. A boy in a Spider-Man T-shirt let out a noisy yawn.

"Come on, weren't you paying attention?" Anthony's voice was turning irritable. "Who knows where bulgur goes?"

A little girl with red braids raised her hand.

Anthony smiled at her. "Yes?"

"I have to go to the bathroom," she said.

Anthony looked exasperated as the teacher beckoned the girl to the front of the room for a hall pass, and two boys in the back row started poking each other in the arm. I shifted in my uncomfortable seat at the back of the room and sneaked a glance at Preston, but he was staring straight ahead. His face was blank, but I was pretty sure that he was thinking the same thing I was: *This is the most boring presentation I've ever heard.* And, personally, I love food. I think it's pretty hard to make it seem boring. I mean, all you have to do to jazz it up is bring in a few apples or something.

"Come on, *bulgur*!" Anthony held up a brochure and waved it at the front row. "Look it up in your pamphlet if you don't know where it goes!"

The boy in the Spidey T-shirt screwed up his face. "What's balrog?"

"Bulgur — it's a *grain*," Anthony snapped.

"Then it goes in the *grain* group," the boy replied. *Like, duh,* his voice seemed to say.

"Yes. Thank you." And then Anthony droned on and on about the importance of whole wheat.

"He still hasn't done *fruits*?" Fiona muttered as Anthony switched topics. "We're going to be here all month." She groaned and put her hands to her temples as if she had a splitting headache. Which maybe she did. She'd barely said a word all afternoon, and her lips seemed locked into a permanent frown. Fiona had even refused to practice the presentation with Preston and me. I wondered if she was still upset about her fight with Jenelle. I knew that I would be, if I were in her situation. But Fiona never acted as if she cared what other people thought.

The two boys in the back row had started tossing wadded-up paper at each other's faces. Preston leaned forward and whispered something to one of them, and he stopped. But I could see that he was still antsy. I didn't blame him. I was getting antsy, too.

Finally, after what seemed like hours, Anthony said, "And now it's time for a little presentation about the dangers of smoking. Let me introduce my assistants, Amy, Preston, and Fiona."

I tried not to roll my eyes at the word "assistants." *Just be grateful he didn't say "servants,"* I told myself. Fiona kept her seat as Preston and I made our way to the front of the class. Preston plugged in an MP3 player as I pulled the hat I'd made out of a brown paper shopping bag. Then I handed the bag to Preston.

Preston's lips twisted into a playful smile, and he whispered, "Ready?"

"Ready," I told him, and I quickly put on the hat. A giggle rippled through the classroom. I had to press my lips together to keep from laughing myself. The hat had an orange crown at the top. A white sheet with three holes — one for the face and two for the arms — hung down from the crown. *Voilà!* I was a cigarette.

Preston hit the PLAY button, and a heavy beat burst from the tiny speakers. I stepped forward and launched into a few of my groove moves, while Preston hit the rap:

"Well, here's a little story that goes to show
What can happen to you when you don't say 'no.'
A boy was hanging with his so-called friend,
He wanted to be cool, so he tried to pretend.
When the friend said, 'Man, do you want a cigarette?'
The boy said, 'Sure! Why not? You bet.'
He puffed on the end, and it made him feel ill,
But his so-called friend said, 'Dude, you look chill.'
So the boy kept smokin' until he could not ignore
That every single day, he wanted to smoke more.
His lungs cried out, they were turning black —
But for this boy, there was just no turning back.

He wanted to quit, but by now he was addicted.
Every time he tried to breathe, his chest felt constricted.
When he tried to talk, all he could do was croak,
And every time he tried to run, he started to choke!
So what should you do when someone offers you tobacco?
Remember they're not your friend — they're just a total wacko."

Preston took the bag and shoved it over my head — "snuffing out" the giant cigarette. I couldn't see anything with that bag over my head, but I could hear the class cheering and clapping wildly. Some of the kids had laughed so hard that they had missed half the rap, so the teacher asked us to do it again. We did, and the class cheered even louder the second time.

"That was great!" Preston said, pulling the bag off of my head. He gave me a high five. The kids were talking and giggling as they gathered up their books and lined up at the door to go to their buses. "This costume is *awesome*."

I felt myself blush a little. "It took about five minutes to make."

Fiona walked up to us. "That's what I like about you, Amy," she said snidely. "You're never afraid to make a fool out of yourself."

"You were terrific." The teacher smiled at us as she herded a few of the kids at the end of the line. "And the food pyramid information was interesting, too," she told Anthony.

"Thanks," Anthony said stiffly.

I hoped he didn't feel too embarrassed about his presentation. After all, it wasn't *bad.* It just wasn't very fun. *Maybe he'll take our idea and turn the whole thing into a skit,* I thought.

"'Remember they're not your friend, they're just a total wacko!'" sang the boy in the Spider-Man T-shirt as the kids tramped out of the room.

The minute they were gone, Anthony turned to us. "What do you think you're doing?" His face was twisted in anger.

I was completely speechless, but Preston just cocked his head slightly. "Teaching kids about the dangers of smoking?"

"That's what *these* are for!" Anthony held up a stack of brochures, then slammed them back on the teacher's desk. "Listen — don't try to be cool. Just read from the brochure."

"But the kids can read it themselves," Preston replied. "When they get home."

"We were just trying to make it interesting," I added.

Fiona sneered. "Oh, it was *interesting*, all right."

Anthony blew out a furious sigh — the kind a bull lets out before it charges at you. "And you're saying that my presentation wasn't interesting? Is that it?" He glared.

Preston and I exchanged a glance. It was clear that neither of us knew how to respond.

"What's that look for?" Anthony demanded. "Are you two questioning my authority?"

"What authority?" Preston asked. I don't think he was trying to be rude — he was really asking. After all, Anthony was just a student, like us. But maybe it wasn't the best thing to say at that moment.

"That's it!" Anthony cried. "I'm calling Allington! You two are getting detention." And he stormed off before we could say anything else.

For the first time all day, Fiona looked delighted. "Way to go, you guys," she said. "I'll be sure to let Dean Denton know that you have a lot of experience with scrubbing and cleaning. Maybe he'll let you do the restrooms!" She flounced away.

"Well, that didn't go exactly the way I'd planned," Preston said after a moment.

I sighed. I wasn't sure about anyone else, but I was getting pretty sick of the HOME.

"Well, hello, derlin'!" The school secretary, Kathy Snell, waved merrily as I stepped into the elegant Allington reception area. "I didn't expect to see you back so soon! And you brought Preston Harringford. Well, now. This must be my lucky day!" She winked at us with heavily mascaraed lashes.

"Hey, Ms. Snell," Preston said, leaning against the glossy dark wood counter. "You're looking especially lovely today."

Ms. Snell let out a high giggle and touched her huge blond hair. "Oh, Preston, you're such a rascal. I love it! What brings you two here?"

I hesitated. Ms. Snell always acted like she was hosting a party for rule breakers. "Um . . . we're actually here to see Mr. Denton," I explained.

"Don't I know it," Ms. Snell said with another broad wink. "But he's fixin' to give a presentation to the department heads this afternoon, so he left word that I was to send you two down to see Chef Boyard to serve your detention. Just have her sign that when y'all are done, okay, sweetheart?" She pointed to the signature line on Mr. Denton's note with a hot-pink fingernail.

I breathed a sigh of relief at not having to see Mr. Denton again. The last time I'd had detention — for accidentally spraying a teacher with a Diet Coke — he'd told me that I was "what was wrong with America."

Chef Boyard was an elegant little woman with her hair in a tidy bun. She didn't look happy when I handed her the note. "This is supposed to make my life easier? Help from a couple of troublemakers?" she asked. Her voice held just a trace of a Cajun accent. She pursed her lips and looked at us doubtfully.

I was about to explain that we weren't really troublemakers, but before I could, Preston had lifted the lid from an enormous pot. "Wow — this smells great!"

"Put that lid back where it came from!" Chef Boyard snapped. She crossed the room in three strides and slammed the lid back into place before Preston could react. "And don't touch anything you're not supposed to, you hear?" She glowered at me, as if she thought I might lunge at one of the other dishes in progress, ruining tomorrow's lunch. "All right, I can see I'll need to give you something simple to do. You can make pudding."

"Great!" I said quickly. I wanted to make up for Preston's mistake. Besides, Allington's pudding was excellent — smooth and rich. "I can't wait to see how you make it."

Chef Boyard fixed us with a glare. "You let the secrets of this kitchen out beyond these walls, and you'll be payin' for it for the rest of your lives. You hear?"

Preston and I looked at each other. "Uh . . . okay," I said.

"Okay what?"

"Okay, we swear that we won't tell anyone how to make the pudding," Preston volunteered.

Chef Boyard seemed to relax . . . slightly. "Good," she said as she tossed each of us an apron.

So naturally, I can't tell you what we did next. I don't know what Chef Boyard had in mind when she said that we would be "payin' for it for the rest of our lives" — and I don't want to find out. I'll just say that the recipe involved eggs, sugar, cream, milk, and the use of a stove. And I don't think I'm revealing too much by telling you that the flavors were vanilla and pistachio.

"That's right." Chef Boyard stood behind Preston as he used a whisk to stir the huge pot on the stove. "Don't stop for even a second!"

She showed us how to ladle the perfect amount of pudding into each individual cup. "Quick wrist," Chef Boyard urged. "Don't let a drop escape!"

Just then, a man in a blue polo shirt and khaki pants appeared in the doorway. He was holding a clipboard. "Chef Boyard?"

"Ah, finally! Let me tell you, Carl — if this week's cherries aren't better than last, you'll be payin' for it for the rest of your life!"

"They're beautiful, I promise," Carl said quickly. "Let me show you the whole delivery."

"I'll be right back," Chef Boyard said. "Just keep pouring that pudding." She started off, then turned sharply and flashed us a warning look. "Don't let me find anything out of place when I get back, or —"

"We'll be paying for it for the rest of our lives?" Preston guessed.

I glared at him. Did he want to get us *another* detention?

"Worse." She narrowed her eyes in a warning. "I'll tell Mr. Denton what I found."

Preston gave me a playful look. "That *is* worse," he said.

I didn't smile, although I have to say that I agreed with him.

We kept on pouring the pudding for a while. Preston was humming the whole time. The humming kept getting louder. I think he might have been trying to get my attention, but I refused to even look up. It was really his fault that we were here in the first place. I didn't want to get in trouble again. My parents would be upset enough as it was.

Finally, Preston stopped humming. "Ahhh . . . ahhh . . . choo!" He let out a huge sneeze. When I looked up, he held up a hand full of green goo. "Mmmm!" he said, licking the green out of his hand and grinning.

"You're deranged," I told him, even though I knew the green stuff was only pudding.

"Oh, come on, try some," Preston said, reaching toward me with a goopy hand.

I let out a shriek and tried to bat his hand away. Unfortunately, I was still holding my ladle. Vanilla splattered across his face.

"You slimed me!" Preston cried, wiping vanilla pudding from his cheek. Grabbing a small spoon, he flicked pistachio pudding at me.

A green splotch landed all over my apron. I couldn't believe it. Now we were definitely going to get in trouble — again! "You are so obnoxious!" I shouted. And then — I swear, I don't know what got into me — I dumped an entire ladleful of vanilla pudding over his head. He hit me with more pistachio, and the fight was on. Cups were overturned, spoons were used as catapults, the floor was covered in sticky slime. The whole thing took only about two minutes, but when we were done, we had a royal mess on our hands and Preston was laughing his head off.

But I wasn't smiling. "Stop laughing!"

"How can I stop laughing when you've got pudding in your hair?" Preston demanded.

"What are we going to do?" I asked as I gaped at the chaos. Chef Boyard would be back any moment.

Preston's laughter evaporated. He looked around, and for the first time, he really seemed to take in the scene around us. "Wow. This was a really bad idea."

"Like most of your ideas," I snapped.

Preston looked hurt, and I immediately regretted what I'd said. After all, it wasn't his fault that Anthony was so unreasonable. "Okay, let's just work as fast as we can," I said finally. "If we get busted, we get busted. But we might as well try."

Preston nodded. "Good thing we have so much practice with cleaning," he said. He gathered up the dirty dishes and washed like mad at the sink while I mopped the floor and wiped down the countertops and walls. Once that was finished, Preston buried our aprons in the dirty linen, and I got out fresh ones. We washed the pudding off of our skin, and I did the best I could to get it out of my hair.

By the time Chef Boyard got back, we were innocently ladling pudding into cups as if nothing had ever happened.

"You're almost finished," she said, nodding in approval. "And it's five o'clock. I can finish up the rest." She reached for Mr. Denton's note.

Preston looked up at me with wide eyes. It had worked! I actually felt myself grinning — I couldn't help it.

"What is this pudding doing here?" Chef Boyard demanded suddenly.

My heart stopped in my chest. I'd missed a spot — we were busted!

But Chef Boyard was just holding up the note. A tiny droplet of vanilla pudding had fallen in the corner. "Very sloppy, Ms. Flowers," she told me. "But — I'll sign it anyway."

And she did. I breathed a huge sigh of relief as I pulled off my apron and dropped it in the dirty linen.

"I can't believe we got away with that," Preston said as we walked out of the kitchen.

"No thanks to you," I told him.

"Me? I'm not the one who still has a blob of pudding in my hair."

I touched my hair. Sure enough, there was pudding caught at the ends. "Oh, well," I said as I put the tip of my hair in my mouth and sucked off the pudding. I guessed it was okay — I'd just washed my hair that morning. And the pudding was delicious.

"Now who's deranged?" Preston asked.

I refused to answer, because it was just too obvious. We both were.

Preston had finally driven me completely crazy.

"Get out! Get out of there!" It sounded like Kirk was trying to kick the bathroom door down. "Some of us have places to go!"

"Just a minute!" I called as I tried to rake a comb through my damp hair. It got halfway down my head, then stuck fast in a mass of curls. Great. I'd already used half a bottle of conditioner on it, but it was really hard to get all of the sticky pudding to dissolve. I blamed the pistachios.

"What are you doing in there?" Kirk demanded. "You've been hogging the bathroom for an hour!" The pounding resumed with new intensity.

"I've been washing pudding out of my hair!" I called as I yanked my T-shirt over my head.

"What?" The pounding stopped for a moment. Then it started up again — double-time. "Don't try to confuse me! Just get out!"

Kirk was mid-pound as I yanked open the door, and he flailed suddenly to avoid punching me in the face. He pointed an accusing finger at me as he staggered back into an upright position. "You're fully dressed!" he cried. "Why didn't you just put on your bathrobe?"

"Do you want me to go back in and change?" I asked him.

Kirk just let out a growl as he shoved his way past me. He shut the door with a bang.

"Amy?" My dad's voice floated up to me on a wave of rosemary and roasting meat. Something delicious was on the grill outside.

I sighed. There was no way to avoid this conversation. "Coming," I called as I headed down the stairs.

I stepped out into our backyard garden, which was blazing with hot-pink azaleas and yellow tulips. Kirk and I are always teasing Mom, telling her that her garden should be on the Azalea Trail, a tour of some of the fanciest private gardens in River Oaks. Of course, our neighborhood, Montrose, isn't quite so fancy. And our garden isn't really that big. But it's as nice as anything else in the city.

Dad was sitting on our stone bench, holding his metal spatula across his lap. He looked like a sentry, watching over the meat on the grill. He didn't smile when he saw me. He just patted the empty space beside him. He sighed as I sat down.

"Oh, Amy," he said. "Another detention."

I nodded. I wanted to tell him how unfair it all was, but I knew it would just sound whiny.

"Do you want to tell me what happened?" Dad asked. His voice was gentle, and I was glad that I was having this conversation with him instead of Mom. She's way harsher.

"I tried to get creative with an assignment," I said. "It seemed like a good idea — but I guess the guy in charge took it the wrong way."

Dad was silent for a while. He stood up to flip the meat, then sat down again. "It's good to be creative," he said at last.

"That's what I *thought*."

"But it's also important to respect authority," Dad went on. "And try to get along with people. Even when they're . . . difficult. What do you think you could have done differently?"

This is *so* my dad. He never tells me what I

should have done. Sometimes I wish he would. I shrugged. "Well, I guess I could have told him exactly what we were planning," I admitted.

Dad tilted his head to look into my eyes. "Maybe next time?" he suggested.

I nodded. "Next time," I promised.

"Because, Amy, you're on a scholarship —"

"I know, I know." One more detention, and my case would come up for review before Headmistress Cardinal. I could be suspended or even permanently expelled. I shuddered, realizing how close I'd come to letting Preston get me into serious trouble this afternoon.

"I know that you're a good student, Amy," my father said at last. "I know you won't let this turn into a problem."

"I won't," I promised, and Dad wrapped a strong, comforting arm around my shoulders.

Dad and I sat there in the quiet garden. The meat hissed on the grill, and I breathed in the rich smell of the beef, and the sweet smell of the flowers around me, and the clean smell of my own shampoo. A fat carpenter bee buzzed around a nearby bush, then crawled into a hole in our wood fence. I wondered if he felt lucky to live in such a pretty garden. I wondered if he appreciated it.

A few moments passed, and then Dad got up to check the grill. "Amy, would you let your mother know that dinner is almost ready? Then would you get the potato salad and the green salad out of the fridge and set the table? Just for three — Kirk isn't eating with us tonight."

"What's he doing?" I asked, just as the front doorbell rang. I hurried to answer it, and when I pulled open the door, I came face-to-face with a gorgeous black-haired girl with high cheekbones and huge, dark eyes. A purple messenger bag was slung across one shoulder.

"Hi — I'm Alizae Khan," she said. She had a sweet smile. "Is Kirk —"

"I'm here I'm here I'm here," Kirk said as his footsteps thudded down the stairs. "Okay, we're adios," he said as he squeezed through the door, his backpack on his shoulder. He was already halfway down the walk before I could even think to ask where he was going.

"We'll eat at Moe's," he called over his shoulder, naming the diner that was walking distance from our house. "Tell Mom and Dad I'll be back by eight thirty."

Alizae gave me a confused smile and turned to follow Kirk. I wanted to tell her not to worry —

that he was always this rude. But it wasn't even true. Kirk was usually pretty good about introducing me to his friends, in spite of the fact that I'm his younger sister. So why was he acting so weird now?

And who was Alizae Khan?

I had a bad feeling that I knew.

CHAPTER SIX

Health Hint:
The average male will eat about fifty tons of food during his lifetime. (About one hundred tons, if it's Preston.)

"Why are these cowgirl cookies so delicious?" I asked as I took another bite. Kiwi, Mitchie, and I were hanging out at the café attached to Divine, Kiwi's parents' shop. "Whenever I try to make cookies, they turn out half burned."

"Aunt Pea does all of the baking," Kiwi said. She sipped her iced tea — it was unsweetened, made with raspberry and mint. Another family recipe. "She's really good."

"Is everyone in your family named after fruits and vegetables?" Mitchie teased.

Kiwi pretended to think it over. "I'll have to ask Uncle Carrot."

Mitchie laughed and tossed a wadded-up napkin at Kiwi's head. Kiwi giggled and ducked.

"So, Amy, are you feeling ready for your big date?" Kiwi asked. She said "big date" in a goofy French accent. "Eet ees tonight, no?"

"Yeah, it's tonight. And I guess I'm ready." I patted the bag at my feet. "Now that I have an outfit." Kiwi and Mitchie had scoured the racks for me, pulling down every halfway decent dress in the place. I'd tried on about sixty outfits, and I had finally ended up with the first thing I'd put on — a pale pink halter dress with white flowers.

The bell over the door jingled, and Jenelle walked into the store. She was carrying an enormous shopping bag, and Linda was with her. She was hauling two huge bags of her own.

"Well, what have you brought us?" Kiwi's mother, Aurora, asked from behind the sales counter. Her brown eyes twinkled and her dimples deepened as Linda and Jenelle started piling clothes and accessories onto the counter. "I always love it when you two clean out your closets! Oh, beautiful," she added as she held up a handbag. Aurora has hair even longer than Kiwi's. She always wears it in a long braid down her back. In her trademark flowing dresses, Aurora looks like the original hippie chick . . . but she's got a real eye for style.

"Hey, Jenelle!" Kiwi cried, flapping like a demented penguin.

Jenelle looked up and smiled. She said something to Linda, who nodded and gave me a friendly wave as Jenelle walked over.

"Hey, y'all," Jenelle said as she plopped down into the chair beside Mitchie. "Mm, looks good." And before I could stop her or cry "NO!!!" she reached over, broke off part of Mitchie's cookie, and popped it into her mouth.

Mitchie slapped her hand lightly, and for a nanosecond I swear I thought they might get into an actual fistfight.

But Jenelle just smiled at her. "Hey! You owe me, remember?"

Mitchie laughed. "You couldn't have eaten that cookie, anyway! It was covered in squirrel drool!"

This made everyone at the table crack up. Everyone except me. I just sat there with a giant invisible question mark hanging over my head. *Mitchie is being friendly to Jenelle? They're sharing cookies? And . . . something about squirrel drool?*

Jenelle was the first to notice my confused smile. "The other day, at our volunteer project, a cookie nearly fell on my head," she explained.

I nodded as if this cleared everything up. "Um."

"It fell out of the tree above her!" Kiwi put in, leaning forward excitedly. "I saw it!"

"What kind of cookie?" I asked.

"Vanilla cream," Jenelle said. "Anyway, Mitchie just grabbed the cookie and tossed it out, and I was like —"

"— she was like, 'Hey! That's *my* cookie! The tree gave it to *me*!'" Mitchie finished, and everyone laughed.

I was still missing something. "So . . . where did the cookie come from?" I asked.

"We had no idea. Kiwi thought Keebler elves, and I said magic tree," Jenelle joked.

I looked at Mitchie, who shrugged. "Cookie fairy was my guess."

"Then one of the garden workers told us that an old lady up the street likes to leave cookies out for the squirrels," Jenelle explained. "They take them, of course, but sometimes they're too big for them to handle."

"So they drop out of the trees," Mitchie explained.

"Wow — that's really . . . weird," I said, and everyone laughed again.

"Hey!" Jenelle said suddenly. "Does anyone want to get their makeup done? Bounce is doing free demonstrations today — the new spring colors are in. Mom and I were about to head over."

"I'm in," Kiwi said, and Mitchie added, "Me too!"

I lifted an eyebrow at her. "You?"

"I can get girly." Mitchie shrugged. "I'm complicated."

"Aren't you coming?" Kiwi asked me. "You're the one with someplace to be tonight."

Jenelle looked at me questioningly, but I didn't feel like getting into the whole Scott-date thing. Instead, I just said, "I can't go. I'm meeting some people here in . . ." I looked at my watch. "Any minute, actually."

Just then, the bell jingled and Fiona strutted in. Her face hardened when she saw Jenelle, but she didn't break her stride as she walked up to our table.

"Hello, Fiona," Mitchie said coldly. "Amy told us she was meeting some people here, but I thought she was talking about *humans*."

Jenelle gave a little giggle-snort. She reached for Mitchie's tea to hide her smile.

"That joke is almost as hilarious as the shirt you're wearing," Fiona shot back, but Mitchie just grinned.

I never, ever thought I'd be happy to see

Preston . . . but when he appeared at the door at that exact moment, I breathed a huge sigh of relief.

"Hey, all the cool cats are here!" he cried as he bounced over to our table and grabbed the seat beside Kiwi.

"Hey, Preston," she said. She pulled her waist-length hair over her shoulder in front of her and toyed with the ends.

"Have you guys been eating cowgirl cookies?" he asked, looking at the plate in front of her. "Oh, man, I'm getting one." He stood up, but Fiona stopped him with a look.

"We've got to work on our final project," she snapped. Her blue eyes glittered dangerously. "We should go to the library."

"Why?" Preston asked. "I'd rather stay here and eat cookies. We can work at that table in the corner."

But apparently Fiona wasn't taking suggestions. She just turned on her heel and strode toward the exit.

"Ooookay," Preston said as the door swung closed behind Fiona. "I guess we're going to the library."

I sighed.

"Just give her what she wants," Jenelle said as she leaned back in her chair. She gave me an even look. "You only have to put up with her for another week."

"Poor Amy," Mitchie said. "Hey, who wants another cookie? Someone stole half of mine."

"I'll take a bite of one," Jenelle joked. "But let me buy."

"Forget it." Mitchie stood up and started toward the cookie counter. "I'll make the squirrel pay me back on Monday!"

Jenelle and Kiwi laughed.

"Well, I guess I'll see you later," I said as I picked up my shopping bag and my backpack. "Have fun at Bounce."

"Don't work too hard," Kiwi called as I started toward the door with Preston. "We'll miss you!"

I smiled at her as Mitchie sat back down beside Jenelle. My three friends leaned their heads together to divide up the cookie. It didn't look like they were going to miss me at all.

"What about jumping jacks?" Preston suggested. "I mean, Anthony can't say no to jumping jacks!"

"Are you kidding?" Fiona snapped. "They'll sound like a herd of elephants on pogo sticks. Why don't we just give each of them a drum set and a megaphone, and call it a day?"

This had been going on for the past twenty minutes. We were sitting at a table near the giant four-story wall of windows in the Allington library. It was a beautiful view that overlooked the brilliant green golf course . . . but it was pretty hard to enjoy it with Preston and Fiona at each other's throats. Preston really wanted to think of a way to make the exercise segment fun for the kids. And Fiona really wanted to go home. So they were having trouble agreeing on a plan.

"Then how about having them run in place?" Preston said.

Fiona scoffed. "I thought you wanted to do something *fun*."

"How about we let the kids come up with a bunch of ideas, and you can shoot them all down? That should be a good workout." There was an edge of anger in Preston's voice.

Fiona sneered, but I cut her off before she could say something dangerous. "Hey, okay, it sounds like we're looking for a fun activity that isn't going to make a lot of noise, right?"

Preston looked over at me, his face saying, *Yeah, so?*

"Well, how about some simple yoga?"

Preston cocked his head, but Fiona let out a snort. "Nobody's doing yoga anymore," she said. "Everyone's into Pilates."

"First graders aren't going to care about what *It!* magazine says is the hottest new exercise, Fiona," Preston said.

Fiona rolled her eyes. "Not *these* first graders."

I guessed that first-grade Fiona would have cared.

"Amy, as usual, you're a genius," Preston said as he stood up. "Thanks for not rubbing it in this time. I'm going to find a book on yoga."

"When do I rub it in?" I called, but he was already walking toward the stacks. I turned to Fiona. "When do I rub it in?"

Fiona just sat there, glowering.

I decided to believe that Preston had just been teasing me. At least I *hoped* he was just teasing.

I took a deep breath. "All right. Maybe we should start thinking about our final project. I was thinking that maybe we could make an interactive model of the cir —"

"Bor-ing," Fiona singsonged.

"Fine. Maybe we could do a presentation on how exercise —"

Fiona rolled her eyes and sighed.

That was it. “What is your problem?” I snapped.

“My problem is that models and presentations are *lame*,” Fiona shot back. “That’s what’s wrong with this entire Health-car-thingie.”

“So why don’t you help us come up with something that isn’t lame?” I demanded. “Instead of just sitting there?”

Fiona studied a fingernail as if there was a microscopic chip in her hot-pink polish. “The whole subject is lame,” she said.

“Listen, Fiona,” I growled. “You’d better get a grip. We’re getting a group grade on this project, and if you sink us, you . . .” I couldn’t really think of a threat that was harsh enough, so I just went with, “You’ll be paying for it for the rest of your life.”

She blinked in surprise. I didn’t blame her. I barely recognized my own voice — it was deep and snarly and, honestly, a little scary. But after a moment, her face settled into a glare. “Why don’t you stop being a goody-goody?” she demanded.

I slammed my hand down on the table with a thud that made Preston’s laptop jump. Even Fiona jumped a little. “Why don’t *you* stop being so obnoxious?” I told her. “Even your so-called friends can’t stand you!”

Fiona gaped at me, her blue eyes wide. For a moment, she didn't say anything, but I saw the tears gathering at the edges of her lids.

My face was on fire, and I instantly regretted what I'd said. Well, *part* of me regretted it. But another part of me was glad. *Fiona thinks she can do whatever she wants, and nobody will ever call her on it.* But people *were* starting to call her on it.

Preston reappeared at that moment with a stack of books. "This looks like a good one. It has lots of pictures." He flipped open the top book and held it out to Fiona. "We could do a couple of these poses, don't you think?"

"Nobody cares what I think," Fiona said, shoving her chair away from the table. Grabbing her bag, she tossed her long, glossy black hair over one shoulder and stood up. "Have fun figuring out the project," she said. Then she stormed out of the library.

Preston looked at me. "Was it something I said?"

"No — something I said," I admitted.

"Really?"

"Don't sound so surprised," I told him. "I can stand up for myself."

"I know, I know, it's just . . ." He shrugged and smiled a little, then looked down at the table.

"What?"

"Well, you're usually so sweet." He looked up at me, and his eyes locked on mine for a moment. Then he looked away.

I'm sweet? I felt all of the blood rush to my head, and my heart stopped. Then it started again, beating madly, as if to make up for lost time. *What's happening?*

I wondered dimly if I was having a heart attack.

"Are you okay?" Preston asked. "You look a little . . ."

"I'm fine," I said, taking the book from him. I nodded. "This looks good. Good idea, Preston."

"It was your idea," Preston reminded me.

"Oh, well." I smiled nervously. "No wonder I like it!" Then I let out this weird squealy nervous laugh, like, "Heeheeheehee!"

Preston looked away, and I put my hands to my head. I didn't know why I was feeling so dizzy all of a sudden.

I only knew one thing — all of this working on health was making me feel kind of sick.

CHAPTER SEVEN

Health Hint:
The human heart weighs less than a pound . . . even when it feels as heavy as a monster truck.

I touched my hair self-consciously as I peered around the huge room, looking for any sign of Scott. I was wearing my new dress, and Mitchie had given me a cool hairstyle, but I still felt underdressed. I mean, I'd had to walk down a red carpet to get to the ballroom, and there was an enormous crystal chandelier hanging from the ceiling. My mom had actually laughed when she dropped me off in our minivan. "Sorry we forgot to hire a limo," she said.

I was just glad that Kirk hadn't come along. I'd never have heard the end of it.

Laughter exploded from a far-off corner of the room. I had to make my way through a sea of ties and tuxedos, but I finally caught a glimpse of a group of eighth-grade guys. Scott was there, holding what looked like a giant super-soaker. When he saw me, he grinned and waved. "Amy, you made it!"

"Uh, yeah," I said. The whole group of eighth-grade guys turned to look at me.

You are so dumb, I thought to myself. All of the air rushed out of my lungs — I had to struggle to breathe. *How could you have thought this was a date? Scott just invited a bunch of friends, that's all.*

A few minutes ago, I'd felt underdressed . . . but in this group of Allington boys, I felt *over*-dressed. I felt my head heat up, like a hot-air balloon. *I wish I could float away. . . .*

"Amy, this is Tom, Derek, Jackson, Miles, Blaine, and Garfield." He waved in the general direction of his friends, and I had no idea who was who — except for the red-haired guy on the end.

"Garfield?" I said. "Are you named after —"

"No, I'm not named after the cat," he snapped, rolling his eyes.

"Oh." I cleared my throat, feeling like an idiot. "Actually, I was going to ask if you were named after the twentieth president of the United States, who was assassinated after only six months in office," I admitted.

The guys behind him cracked up, and two of them high-fived. "She got you, bro!" one of them shouted, punching Garfield in the arm.

"Yeah," Garfield said, looking about as surprised as if I'd just pulled an elephant out of my ear. "Um, yeah, he's a distant relative or something."

"Hey, Amy, want to try the game?" Scott gestured to the setup in front of him. It was amazing — the aliens were three-dimensional holograms, and practically life-sized. Super-cool. It looked like you were really *in* the game.

"Man, girls don't like games with aliens," said one of the guys — Jackson, I think.

"Oh, please." I took the alien-zapper right out of his hands. I pressed a purple button and a crowd of bug-eyed aliens raced toward me. *Zap! Zap! Zap!* Three green space creatures disintegrated right before my eyes.

"Whoa!" Scott looked impressed. "I didn't know you were into video games!"

"Eh, I've got a fifteen-year-old brother," I explained, handing the zapper back to Jackson.

"Come on, Amy, let me show you around a little." Scott gave his alien-zapper to Garfield and touched my elbow gently. His fingers were warm on my arm as he led me to a few of the different displays. "My dad's company is trying to become the next wave in gaming," Scott explained. "They think people are going to go nuts for the holograms."

"It seems even more interactive than a screen," I agreed, trying to sound enthusiastic. Of course, the games were totally amazing . . . but I was still trying to get over the fact that this wasn't exactly the date I'd pictured. In fact, I could totally imagine my brother enjoying this non-date more than I was. *Kirk would die of joy if he were here,* I thought as I watched a guy demonstrate a holographic ninja game.

Scott stopped suddenly, and looked at me with those velvety brown eyes. "I'm really glad you could come tonight," he said.

My mouth went dry. I felt as if I'd tried to eat a pillow. "You — you are?"

He nodded slowly, and his smile made my knees feel like I was standing on Jell-O. "Listen, do you want to —"

"Scottie boy, there you are!" A heavyset man with white hair and a nose like a potato clapped him on the back. "Your father wants you to demonstrate the helicopter!"

"Oh, sure, Mr. Robertson," Scott said. "It's Dad's latest game," he explained quickly. "Be back soon, okay?"

"Okay." Mr. Robertson was already steering him away. I sighed. *Wow. This date sure is romantic,* I thought sarcastically. I looked around at the various displays. *Now what?* I was tempted to leave, even though Scott had said he'd be back. . . . But who knew how soon was "soon"?

"Amy? Hey, Amy!" Anderson was trotting over, wearing a huge smile. "I never expected to see you here! Isn't this stuff awesome?"

I grinned. The one person who could help me make lemonade out of my lemons had just arrived. "I didn't know you'd be here, either. Do you know Scott?"

"Who?"

"Scott Lawton? He goes to our school."

Anderson thought it over. "Yeah, I think I met him once, but I don't really know him. I'm here because my mom's an investor in this company. Hey, have you had the chocolate-covered strawberries? They're *so* good. Come on!" Anderson practically dragged me toward the refreshments. But I stopped about ten feet from the table.

"Oh, ugh," I said. "Look who's lurking by the mini-pastries."

"Change of direction," Anderson said as he steered me toward the drink table instead. "I do *not* want to see Fiona right now."

I looked over my shoulder. That was her, all right. She was nibbling a carrot and scowling. "She looks like she's in an even worse mood than usual."

Anderson handed me a glass of sparkling water. "She and Jenelle are still —" He made a face and ripped at the air with clawlike fingers.

I shook my head. "Fiona still hasn't apologized?" *Why am I surprised?* I wondered. Fiona would probably sprout a unicorn horn before she would ever say, "I'm sorry."

Anderson sighed. "You know, I really don't get it. I like Fiona. Even after what she did, I still understand why she and Jenelle are friends. I just don't understand why Fiona doesn't like *me*." He looked at me with his huge blue eyes. His feelings were hurt, I could tell. But I didn't know what to say to him that would make him feel better. The fact was, Fiona *didn't* like him. And there wasn't much anyone could do about it.

"Hey, listen — let's try one of these cool games," I said quickly. I placed both of our glasses on a nearby platter and grabbed his hand. "We can't tell everyone at school that we came to this party and just stood around, drinking seltzer."

"Which game?" he asked.

"How about this one?" I stopped in front of a

display. Different-sized holographic cubes slid across the floor, and loud dance music was pumping. "What is this game, anyway?" I asked the gorgeous blond woman standing beside the controls.

"It's called Dance Break," the woman explained. "When the music starts, you have to follow the lead dancer while avoiding the cubes. Basically, it's a dancing obstacle course."

"Sounds great," I said, but Anderson shook his head.

"No way," he said. "I didn't come here to humiliate myself."

"Of course, Amy loves to humiliate herself wherever she goes," said a nasty voice behind me. Fiona was sneering at me, staring daggers with her blue cat eyes.

Great. She found us. *Why does she always have to appear at the worst possible moment?* I wondered. *Why can't she just stand in the corner eating cheese cubes like a normal person and leave me alone?* "Don't worry, Fiona. I can dance."

"Right." Fiona smirked. "You'll fall on your rear before the end of Round One."

She was starting to work my nerves. "Well, if you're so sure that's what's going to happen, why don't you come up here and join me?" I said.

Fiona barked a laugh. "I'm the best dancer at Allington," she announced. "Everyone knows that."

Actually, I *had* heard something like that. But I really didn't care. I cocked my head. "Then prove it."

Fiona looked like she might refuse, but Anderson said, "Don't do it, Fiona. Jenelle told me that Amy's an amazing dancer."

I looked at Anderson. *When did Jenelle ever say that?* I wondered. I didn't think I'd ever danced in front of her.

But that was all Fiona needed to hear. She shot him a furious glare, then in one quick move, she stepped up to the podium and pushed the START button. In a moment, new music pulsed through the speakers, and a handsome guy in jeans and a white T-shirt appeared. He was the hologram, and we were supposed to follow his moves.

The game started out slow — step to the right, step to the left, step to the front, that kind of thing. And the bouncing holographic cubes didn't come too close. By the end of Round One, I was barely breathing hard. Neither one of us was out.

"Hope it's not too challenging for you," Fiona said, glancing my way.

"Bring it," I told her.

In Round Two, things got interesting. The lead dancer threw in a few turns, and the music picked up. In Round Three, there were leaps, and the cubes began their real attack. If you followed the hologram's dance moves perfectly, you wouldn't touch them.

"Whoa!" I cried as a blue cube sheared a little close during a leap-turn combination.

Fiona barely avoided a flying purple cube — her arm was a little off.

Anderson let out a piercing whistle and a few people clapped as we danced our way through Round Eight. The music was pulsing, and I felt the sweat pouring down my face. We had to pop and lock, and there were some wild martial arts moves I'd never seen before. I had to admit one thing — Fiona was an incredible dancer. She hit a triple turn at the end of Round Ten — enough for one hundred bonus points. "That's what ten years of ballet can do."

I nailed a somersault and leaped back onto my feet. "And that's ten years of jazz and hip-hop," I said without missing a beat.

The crowd that had gathered let out a cheer, and Anderson whistled so loud that I thought he might break the glasses on the drink table.

In Round Thirteen, Fiona let out a little shriek

as we had to lean into a back bend to avoid a yellow cube. I popped right back up, but Fiona was a beat late. Without thinking, I grabbed her wrist and pulled her back to her feet. We both hit the next move just in time, then leap, leap, roll across the floor, and turn, kick, bow.

Another level. Then another. I was getting tired, but when I looked over at Fiona, she actually smiled at me. "You're not bad, Flowers," she said during a brief pause between rounds.

I was too out of breath to reply. I just had time to inhale, then we were moving again. I hadn't taken a dance class in a few months, and my muscles were aching, straining with each move. Still, I was having fun. And Fiona seemed to be, too.

"I can't believe it!" the blond woman said into the microphone at the end of the final round. "These girls have completed Round Twenty — they beat the game!"

"We beat the game!" Fiona cried, and she pulled me into a hug. "We beat it!"

I stood there, dripping like a cold soda on a hot day and hugging Fiona while a crowd of people I didn't know clapped and cheered. *This is one of the top-five weirdest moments of my life,* I thought. I was wiped out — I could hardly breathe.

Fiona's chest was heaving, too, and for a minute I thought she might be crying, but when she pulled away, I saw that she was laughing. "Are you thinking what I'm thinking?" she asked, her blue eyes shining.

"Are you thinking that you might collapse from exhaustion?" I asked.

"No," she said with a laugh. "I'm thinking that this game is the answer to Preston's prayers!"

"Preston?" I said, but Fiona had already darted over to talk to the blond woman, and then I felt someone tap me on the shoulder.

"Amy?" It was Scott. "That was amazing!"

"Oh, thanks!" I said as I tried to shove my sweaty, limp hair out of my face and pat it back into something resembling a hairstyle. "Um — how did the helicopter thing go?" I tried to ignore the fact that my pink-and-white dress was sticking to my skin.

Scott winced. "Listen, that's what I came to tell you. My dad really wants me to demonstrate a few of the games for his investors —"

I wasn't sure whether I should feel disappointed or relieved. "Oh, no problem," I said quickly. "You just — just — go ahead and . . ."

"Listen, Amy." Scott grabbed my hand and I tried really hard not to think about how sweaty and gross it was. He tucked a stray strand of hair behind my ear. "I'm really sorry. This kind of isn't how I pictured this night going. . . ."

"It isn't?" Our eyes locked, and warmth spread all over my body.

"Scott!" shouted Mr. Robertson. He waved impatiently.

"Be right there!" Scott called over his shoulder. He looked down at me and gave my hand a squeeze. "I'll — I'll see you at school, okay?"

"Okay." I nodded.

He nodded, too. Then we stood there for a moment, before he darted away.

"Amy, that was great!" Anderson said as he came up to me. "Here, have some water, you must be dying of thirst. I can't believe you and Fiona and that game!" he gushed. "You totally blew my mind!"

I laughed as I took a sip of water. It was the most delicious water I'd ever tasted in my life. I glanced over at Fiona, then at Scott's retreating form. "That's the thing about this whole party," I admitted. "It's totally mind-blowing."

"Something smells good in here," I said as I walked into Jenelle's kitchen the next day. A sweet, chocolatey scent had hit my nose before I was halfway up the front walk. Jenelle had invited me over to help make dessert for the local homeless shelter, and — judging by the smell — she was going all out. "What's on the menu?"

"Kiwi's teaching us her aunt's secret recipe for triple-chocolate-chunk cupcakes," Jenelle explained from her place behind the counter. She was stirring thick batter in a yellow bowl.

"White chocolate, milk chocolate, and dark chocolate chips with chocolate frosting." Kiwi winked. "It's a killer. One of the bestsellers at the café."

"And do you charge extra if someone wants to wear some of the batter on their nose?" I asked, looking at Jenelle. She had a chocolate splotch smeared near her cheek.

"What?" Jenelle said, touching the side of her nose. Her eyes widened and locked on to Mitchie, who was opening a bag of chocolate chips while looking as innocent as possible. "Mitchie!"

"Amy!" Mitchie said, tossing a kitchen towel at my head. "You're ruining the payback!"

Kiwi dissolved into giggles as Jenelle wiped the chocolate off of her face. "I can't believe this!" Jenelle said. "I *told* you — I thought you knew that you had mulch in your hair!"

"And I thought you *wanted* that chocolate on your nose!" Mitchie crowed, grinning.

"Um, what are we talking about?" I asked as I sat down on one of the tall stools at the counter.

Kiwi passed me a bowl and a whisk. "Oh, Jenelle let Mitchie have a whole conversation with the woman who runs the community garden and didn't tell her that she had a huge chunk of bark in her hair. It was hilarious."

I nodded. "Got it."

Mitchie smiled apologetically. "It was a location situation."

"A what?"

"You had to be there," Jenelle explained.

"Okay! So, Amy, you can do the frosting," Kiwi said, handing me a recipe. "The powdered sugar and butter are here, and you can melt the chocolate chunks in this Pyrex bowl in the microwave. . . ."

"Look at the organizationista!" Mitchie laughed.

"Do you have any marigolds for us?" Jenelle asked, and the three of them cracked up. Again.

I shifted in my seat, feeling my smile frozen on my face. I looked from Jenelle to Mitchie and back again, but nobody bothered explaining the marigolds comment. I guess it didn't really matter. I was sure that it was another location situation.

It was a little weird to have my friends acting so buddy-buddy. I mean, in one way it was great. At least it wasn't Icebergville between Mitchie and Jenelle anymore. Then again, it was a little weird to feel so . . . left out.

"So, how many cupcakes do we need to make?" I asked, hoping to have a subject that we could all talk about.

"Fifty," Mitchie said. "The shelter gives out fifty full dinners every night — appetizer, salad, main course, two side dishes, and dessert."

"And why are we doing this again?" I measured four cups of powdered sugar into the bowl. "I thought you were volunteering for a garden."

"We're helping out Lucia," Jenelle explained. "She's got a different group of volunteers making each dish. Besides, the shelter is across the street from the garden."

"Lucia?" I said, looking over at Mitchie. *Don't tell me that they're best friends now, too,* I thought.

But Mitchie just rolled her eyes. "It's for a good cause?" she said in Lucia's trademark question-mark style. "And we'll get extra credit?"

"And it involves cupcakes?" Kiwi joined in.

"I wonder what dish Fiona is making," Mitchie said mischievously, sneaking a glance at Jenelle.

Jenelle snorted. "Right."

"So, Amy, how was your *date*?" Mitchie fluttered her eyelashes at me.

"Omigosh, I can't believe you let us go on and on about mulch!" Jenelle gushed. "I forgot last night was the big night — tell all!"

"Eh." I put the chocolate chips in the microwave and pressed START. "The party was really cool, and the games were amazing. But it turns out it wasn't a date — Scott had invited all of his friends along, too."

"What?" Kiwi shrieked. "He made you get a new dress for *that*?"

"Guys can be so weird," Mitchie said, popping a white chocolate chip into her mouth.

"Speaking of weird," I began, and I told them all about the dance-off with Fiona. I got really excited, describing how the music got more intense and the dancing got harder as we went up the levels. "And at the end, she swooped me into this huge hug! And I think she's planning some kind of dance routine for the kids in the health program. Which would be great, because she's been kind of a pain, and we all need to work together on the final project."

Jenelle and Mitchie exchanged a long glance.

"What?" I asked.

"It's just that — " Jenelle shook her head. Right then, the timer went off. She grabbed an oven mitt and turned to take the cupcakes out of the oven.

"It's just that you shouldn't put too much faith in Fiona," Mitchie said, looking me in the eye.

"It's not like we're becoming friends, or anything," I told her. I knew that I sounded defensive, but I couldn't help it. "She was just — nice. For once in her life. We had fun."

"And maybe she'll come through for the final project," Kiwi suggested, and I nodded.

Jenelle didn't say anything.

Michie bit her lip. "Yeah, maybe."

But she didn't sound like she believed it. I didn't blame her. I wasn't sure I believed it, either. Then again, the look in Fiona's eyes when we won the game had been different from anything I'd seen before. She actually looked — happy.

I thought about her expression when I'd said that her own friends couldn't stand her, and after her fight with Jenelle. There had been tears in her eyes.

It was strange to think about, but I was actually starting to suspect that Fiona just might have . . . *feelings.*

CHAPTER EIGHT

Health Hint:
You can burn off about one hundred calories in ten minutes by dancing . . . with or without a hologram.

"No way." Preston shook his head and folded his arms across his chest. He looked like a locked building.

"Way!" Fiona cried. She waved at the video game setup as if she were a game show hostess showing off a gleaming new car. "I know, isn't it great?"

I shook my head in disbelief. "They aren't even selling these yet." I trailed my fingers over the plastic covering the brand-new controls. *Fiona must have gotten to the classroom super-early to set this thing up,* I realized. *And she must have had a whole team of people with her.*

"Yeah, but I convinced them to let us use it because it's for such a good cause." Fiona's blue eyes were brilliant. "And, of course, my parents own a big chunk of the company. But anyway, isn't this great? Preston, it's just what you were looking for!" She pressed a button, and dance music pulsed through the speakers.

"What *I* was looking for?" Preston repeated, shouting a little to be heard over the music. He threw up his arms, and his tie flapped up with them. "I just thought we should do some yoga! Something simple, Fiona. Something that wouldn't make a lot of noise, *remember*?"

Fiona looked shocked. Her face turned white, then red, as if someone had slapped her across the cheeks. "Are you kidding me?" she screeched. "This game is *amazing*! The kids are going to go nuts!"

"*Anthony* is going to go nuts," Preston shot back. He hit the POWER button, shutting off the music. Silence rang through the classroom.

"Amy," Fiona said, turning to me. "Would you please explain to Preston that this game is the coolest thing since the last Ice Age?"

"It's cool," I promised.

"Amy, would you please tell Fiona that I'm not

about to spend the afternoon in a hot kitchen making pudding?" Preston demanded.

"What does *pudding* have to do with anything?" Fiona cried.

But, of course, I knew exactly what Preston was talking about. This game had Major Anthony Freak-out written all over it. "We should probably let Anthony know about it," I suggested. "Before we just go ahead."

"I already told the principal," Fiona insisted. "They said that the idea was 'very creative and an exciting insight into health and fitness.'"

I thought about my promise to my dad. Something told me that Anthony wouldn't be happy if we just went over his head and got the principal's permission. "But we should probably let him know, anyway."

"Great, Amy — thanks," Fiona said. She smiled at me.

For a nanosecond, I thought she was being sarcastic. Like, *Thank you soooo much for not backing me up.* But then I realized that she thought I'd just volunteered to go talk to Anthony. I was about to explain that I thought Fiona would be a better person to do the talking when Preston said, "Fine, Amy will see what he has to say."

I sighed. Okay. It looked like this was officially *my* job. I trudged up the hall to the small office that Anthony and Ms. Greene were using while we were at the school. Ms. Greene was just closing the door behind her as I walked up. "Anna! So good to see you! How are you enjoying your time with us at Health on the Move?"

"Um . . ." I hesitated a minute — I wasn't sure whether I should bother to tell her that my name wasn't Anna, but then I decided it didn't really matter. "We're all having a great time," I said. A small lie, but I didn't blame myself too much. "Er, Ms. Greene, I was just about to let Anthony know that one of the other volunteers has brought in a video game for the kids to try."

Ms. Greene frowned. "A video game?"

"It's a dancing video game," I explained. "They'll get lots of exercise, and we thought it would be fun and different."

"Oh, that sounds fantastic! I'm sure Tony will be thrilled. He adores video games, and — you know — he's always trying to think of fun new ideas to get the children interested in health. He's in the office now, practicing his speech about the circulatory system!" She beamed. "Now, I'm off to meet with the fifth-grade teachers. We're developing a curriculum for older children. Have a wonderful day! Ta-ta!"

I hope the curriculum doesn't involve more circulatory system speeches, I thought as I knocked lightly on the door. I heard Anthony say, "Enter," so I pushed open the door.

"Chamber of the heart — what are you doing?" Anthony snapped as I poked my head inside. "Can't you see I'm busy?" He was standing beside a desk, holding a large stack of paper.

"Oh — sorry — I thought I heard you say 'Enter.'"

"What?" Anthony glanced at his notes. "Oh. I guess I did say that the blood *enters* the chamber of the heart. . . ."

I cleared my throat. "Uh, well, as long as I'm here . . ." I quickly explained about the game.

Anthony barely looked up from his papers. "Fine, fine. Nobody cares about the exercise portion, anyway."

"Okay," I said. "Great! See you later." I closed the door and left him to his circulatory system.

Preston still didn't seem thrilled about the game, but Fiona was thrilled enough for all of us. "Okay, we still have an hour before the kids come back from music class," Fiona said. "We should practice the presentation. I was thinking that I could explain the game quickly and just talk about the benefits of exercise. I have a chart here—" She had hooked up her laptop to a large screen, and at the touch of a button, a PowerPoint display popped up. "Then you guys could demonstrate the game."

"I think I'd rather give the talk," Preston said quickly.

Fiona rolled her eyes. "Don't be such a sore loser," she told him. "I practiced the speech all day yesterday. All *you* have to do is follow the holographic dancer in Round One—it's easy." She pushed the button, and the music started again. The holographic dancer appeared. "Hey, are you ready to dance?" he demanded.

Preston looked at me, and I shrugged my shoulders. "We're getting a grade on this," I reminded him.

He blew out a frustrated sigh. "Fine," he snapped.

Fiona pressed PLAY. The cubes bounced around, but they were nowhere near us as the dancer started to move. Step to the right, step to the left, step to the front. . . . But something was wrong. First, Preston stepped left three beats too late. "Oof, sorry!" he said as he ran into me. He tried to step forward, but a holographic cube was in the way. He did a weird little jog-and-flail to the right, and nearly ran into me again. Unfortunately, I was in the middle of a simple turn, and I kind of — tripped him.

"Ow!" Preston cried as he went down — hard. "My ankle!"

Fiona shut off the music as Preston writhed on the floor.

"Are you okay?" I asked, reaching for his foot.

"Don't touch it!" he shouted, slapping my hand away. "I told you this was a stupid idea!" He tried to move his foot, and winced in pain.

"I — sorry —"

"You could have mentioned that you're the world's worst dancer," Fiona put in.

Preston glared at her. "Don't help me," he said as he struggled to get up. Unfortunately, he fell back on his butt. "Ow!"

"What's going on?" Anthony cried as he rushed into the room. He gaped at the video game setup, then reached down to help Preston to his feet. "What's all this stuff? What do you three think you're doing?"

Fiona stared at me.

A cold wave washed over me. *Did Anthony seriously not even remember that we'd talked this morning?* "We — I told you that there was a game —"

"You didn't tell me that it was *dangerous*," Anthony snapped. "You didn't tell me that I'd be dealing with injuries!"

"I'm fine," Preston said as he limped toward the door. He took another step and grimaced in pain.

"Wait — where are you going?" Anthony demanded.

Preston didn't even look back. "To the school nurse," he said.

"Great. Now I have to take over the health unit, too?"

"Fiona and I can handle it," I said.

"You've *handled* it already," Anthony snarled as he headed toward the door. "I'm calling Mr. Denton. This is ridiculous!"

"But what about the game?" Fiona asked.

"Get rid of it!" Anthony yelled. He looked at me with narrowed eyes. "I want it *gone* by the time I get back!" He slammed the door as he left.

"How did this get to be my fault?" I asked nobody in particular.

Fiona laid a gentle hand on my arm. "Don't worry about it," she said. "It was an accident.

Anthony's just freaking out because he's the one who said it was okay."

"I guess." But I had a bad feeling that Anthony wouldn't put it that way when he called Allington. "If I get another detention, I'll be in serious trouble," I admitted. "I'll have to go before the review board. . . ."

Fiona held up her manicured hand. "Not going to happen."

"But he's going to call —"

"*Not* going to happen," she repeated. "Listen, you have witnesses. Preston and I both know that Anthony said it was okay to use the game. We'll back you up."

"You . . . will?"

Fiona smiled. "Yeah. Of course," she said. "Personally, I hope he *does* call the school. I can't stand that guy. I can't wait to tell Mr. Denton the whole story."

"What if he doesn't listen to you?"

"Please. My parents gave the school the money to renovate the auditorium last year." She gave me a don't-mess-with-this grin. "Believe me, they'll listen."

I laughed. For the first time, I was starting to see what people liked about Fiona.

* * *

I clicked on my buddy list for the fiftieth time. None of my friends were online. *Where is everybody?* I wondered. *I need help!*

My mother stood at the kitchen counter, chopping an onion and humming a song that sounded vaguely familiar. It was probably something I'd heard on the radio. Mom has a habit of listening to Top Forty stations, then humming the music in a way that makes it sound like it's coming from an elevator. She can take the All-American Rejects and turn them into a trip to the orthodontist's waiting room. Normally, I think it's kind of funny, but today it was making me nervous. I couldn't decide whether or not to tell her about my possible detention. After all, I hadn't *officially* heard from the school. And Fiona had said not to worry — that she'd fix it. *Maybe she will.* I mean, it was *possible.*

Then again, Anthony had been *furious*. And Ms. Greene seemed to think that Anthony walked on vitamin water. I wondered whether she would remember that I told her about the video game . . . or if she would insist that I must not have informed Anthony of my crazy scheme.

And Anthony wasn't my only problem. Preston was fuming, too. Not that I blamed him. I mean, he was injured, and then Fiona had to make fun of his dancing. . . .

But I wasn't sure whether or not to apologize. *What would I even apologize for?* All I knew was that Preston didn't speak to me for the rest of the day. He wouldn't even look in my direction. I used to think that all I wanted was for him to leave me alone. But now that he was leaving me alone, I felt . . . well . . .

I don't know. I kind of missed him, I guess.

I need to talk to someone. I grabbed the cordless from the wall and punched in Mitchie's number.

"Hello?"

"Hey, Mitchie, it's Amy. Do you —"

"Hello?" Her voice was choppy, and I thought I could hear laughter in the background. "Hello? I can barely hear you."

"Mitchie, it's Amy."

"Amy! Oh, hey! Listen, I —" Her words completely dropped out for a moment, then resurfaced with "— call you back later?"

Disappointment wrapped around me like a heavy blanket. I hesitated a moment. I really wanted someone to talk to — there was too much buzzing around in my head. But what could I do? Demand that Mitchie give me advice over a bad cell phone connection? I'd just have to call Kiwi or Jenelle. "Sure," I said finally.

"Great. We're almost done —" I heard giggles and Mitchie said, "Hey, guys, just a sec — I'm on the phone with Amy."

Someone squealed, and a voice yelled, "Hi, Amy!"

"That was Kiwi," Mitchie explained. "Jenelle is waving at the phone. She can't *see* you, Jenelle." More laughter.

I felt my chest sink like a pebble in a lake. "Where are you guys?"

"We're at Teas," Mitchie said, naming one of the nicest nurseries in Houston. "We're buying some plants —" She broke up again. "— garden project." There was another short silence, and then, "— tried to call earlier, but you don't have a cell."

"Oh." I wanted to say something else. Something like, "Well, why didn't you leave a message at my house?" but my throat was too tight. I couldn't get anything out. Besides, I knew it was silly. By the time I got the message and found a ride to Teas, it would have been time for them to leave.

"Hello? Hello? Listen, I can't hear you. We'll talk later, okay?"

"Yeah, sure." It was a whisper, but it didn't matter because we got cut off. Carefully, I placed the phone back in the receiver, then I looked down at my laptop screen. I didn't have anyone to call.

My mother stopped humming and looked at me through her square glasses. "Are you okay, honey?"

"Yeah," I said quickly. "Sure."

"You seem —" Mom shook her head, smiling a little. "Not like yourself."

"I'm okay. You need some help?" I shoved my chair away from the table and walked over to the counter.

"Oh, your dad asked me to cut up these veggies for kebabs," Mom said. "Do you want to put them on skewers? They have to marinate for a couple of hours before dinner."

"Dad's been the Grillmaster lately," I said as I speared a large cherry tomato.

"I'm not complaining," Mom said with a smile.

"Me neither," I agreed. Honestly, everything my dad makes is delicious. And my dad makes everything.

There was a tap at the back door, and Alizae Khan smiled at us through the screen.

"Alizae!" My mother hustled to the door, wiping her hands on a kitchen towel. "How are you?"

"I'm fine, thanks, Mrs. Flowers," Alizae said as she stepped into the kitchen. "Hi — Amy, right? We didn't officially meet."

I waved at her with a kebab. "Hi."

Mom looked up the rear stairs. "Does Kirk know —"

"I'm right here," Kirk said, thundering down the steps. "Hey, Alizae. I thought we could study in my room."

"Would you two like some strawberry pie?" Mom offered. "I think we still have some from last night."

"I ate it," Kirk said. "Come on, Alizae."

I rolled my eyes. *Mr. Romance.* I hoped Alizae wasn't his girlfriend — for *her* sake.

"Well, have an apple or something," Mom said. "It's a long way off until dinner. Now, what have we got? I think we have some raspberry iced tea. How does that sound?"

"That sounds wonderful," Alizae said. She turned toward my mother, and she didn't see Kirk shifting nervously from one foot to another. He looked panicked, like he might jitter down the block at any second.

Mom made a plate of sliced apple and cheese (Mom doesn't cook, but she's okay at slicing) and poured iced tea for Alizae and me. Kirk refused to eat or drink anything, and looked like he might leap up from the kitchen table at any moment.

"So, what are you guys studying?" I asked as I speared a chunk of onion.

Kirk glared at me and mouthed, "Don't even." I had no idea what that was all about.

Alizae looked at Kirk. "Geometry," he snapped. "It's really hard, okay?"

I didn't even have time to process how weird that was, because just then someone else knocked at the back door and Mitchie called, "Hey, Amy!"

"Hey! Come in!"

"Kirk!" Mitchie said happily as she yanked open the door. "I'm so glad you're here because —" She stopped when she caught sight of Alizae, and Mitchie's smile did a jerky little up-and-down dance, like it couldn't decide whether or not it wanted to stay put on her face. "Oh, hi."

Alizae was chewing her apple, so she couldn't speak.

"This is Alizae," my mother said. "Kirk's . . . uh . . ." Mom looked at Kirk. ". . . friend." She said "friend" like she wasn't really sure.

Alizae waved, and Mitchie nodded at her.

"What's up?" Kirk asked.

"Oh, uh . . ." Mitchie gave her head a little shake, like she needed to rattle her brain back into place. "Uh . . . I just — I have this." She handed him a small neon-green postcard.

"Skate rally!" Kirk said, reading the postcard. "Awesome! It's this weekend. Are you going?"

"Uh, yeah," Mitchie said. "Yeah, I'll be there."

"Cool." Kirk glanced at Alizae. "I — I think I can make it. It kind of depends . . ."

"Oh." Mitchie just stood there for a moment, and none of us said anything. "Well! I should get going. I . . . uh . . . I just . . ." She turned to me. "You sounded a little . . ." Her voice trailed off. "I guess maybe it was the cell phone."

No! I wanted to say. *No! I need to talk to you!* But I couldn't just keep her here with Kirk and Alizae in the same room. *Mitchie probably needs to talk to someone as badly as I do,* I realized. *But not here. Not now.* "Call me later, okay?" I asked.

"Yeah." Mitchie nodded, then her eyes flicked to Alizae. "Nice to meet you," she said.

"You too!" Alizae chirped.

Mitchie gave Kirk a little wave and walked out the door.

Great, I thought. I glanced at Kirk, who was watching Alizae eat with a strange expression on his face. It just didn't seem fair. *My friend came over to cheer me up, and now we all feel worse than before.*

CHAPTER NINE

Health Hint:
There is enough pressure in the human heart to squirt blood up to thirty feet. (Don't think about that too much.)

"Your problems are officially over." That was the first thing Fiona said to me when she came up to my locker the next morning. "I took care of everything."

"Yeah, as usual?" Lucia put in. She was right behind Fiona — naturally — typing something on her purple cell phone. She didn't even look up.

"You mean, with Anthony?" I asked as I pulled my Texas history book from the shelf. "Are you serious?" My heart gave a flutter.

"Are *you* serious?" Lucia shot back, eyeing the mirror stuck to the inside door of my locker.

The frame was fake fur — green with yellow polka dots.

"Did you make that thing?" Fiona asked.

"It's, like, obvious?" Lucia said-slash-asked, typing away on the cell again.

"Yeah, I made it."

I expected one of those Fiona slice-and-dice insults — something like, "I pity the Muppet that had to give its life for your weird decorating ideas," but she just said, "Amy Flowers, you are a trip." She flipped her long black hair behind her shoulder. "And yes, everything with Anthony is locked down." She gave a tight little smile. "Daddy had a long chat with Mr. Denton last night."

"Wow . . . thanks." I didn't know what to say. On one hand, I was incredibly grateful that I didn't have a third detention. On the other hand — well, I couldn't help thinking that this little chat might lead to some bigger problems. I wasn't sure Anthony would appreciate Mr. Von Steig's phone call. *What am I going to say to him when I see him this afternoon?* I wasn't looking forward to it.

"Oh, and here," Fiona said. She fluttered her perfect manicure in Lucia's general direction.

"It's programmed?" Lucia said, handing me the cell phone.

I just stood there, looking down at the purple case. It was a brand-new Taffy. I'd seen the ads on TV, but had never actually seen one up close. "Wow, nice phone," I said, feeling as if I was missing something.

Fiona stood there as if she expected me to say something else.

"Um, do you need me to hold it for you or something?" I asked. "I have plenty of space in my bag." Of course, my bag always has so much junk in it that I couldn't guarantee that I'd be able to find it again when Fiona needed it.

Lucia rolled her eyes. "You are so clueless?"

Fiona smiled. "It's actually kind of cute," she said.

"That's what I meant?" Lucia added quickly.

"Amy — the phone is for you," Fiona explained. "So we can keep in touch. We still have a lot of planning to do for the final project. I know you don't have one, so. . . ." She shrugged.

"For *me*?" My voice was as squeaky as a sneaker soaked with water as I touched the phone's glossy face.

Fiona laughed. "I thought purple was the most *you*. But maybe you can hot glue some fake fur to the sides or something."

"No — no way. I *love* it! But . . ." I hesitated.

Fiona lifted her dark eyebrows, as if to say, "And?"

". . . my parents kind of don't want me to have a cell phone," I explained.

Lucia made a *phish* sound, and Fiona said, "The first year is paid for. Unlimited calling and texting."

I looked down at the phone, still unsure. I wasn't certain that money was the reason my parents didn't want me to have a cell phone. Then again, the phone was a gift. And my mother had told me to always accept gifts graciously — even ones you didn't like or need.

Besides, I couldn't stop the little voice in my mind that whispered: *And if you'd had a cell phone yesterday, Mitchie would have called you, and you would have spent the afternoon with your friends. . . .*

"Okay," I said at last. I silently vowed to tell my parents all about it — later. "Okay. Great! Thanks!" I leaned forward and hugged Fiona. For a minute, she stood there like a goalpost. Then she seemed to realize what was happening, and she hugged me back.

"You're welcome." She sounded surprised. "I mean, it's not like I got you a car or anything."

"It's better," I said warmly.

"And I loaded all of our numbers into it already?" Lucia volunteered.

"Wow, this is really weird." Mitchie appeared suddenly. She lifted an eyebrow at Fiona and me, and that was when I realized I was still holding Fiona's hand. "Is it opposite day or something?"

Fiona flicked her fingers, dislodging my hand. "I guess that would explain why you're wearing a skirt," she snapped at Mitchie.

"I think Mitchie looks fantastic," Jenelle said, walking up behind Mitchie. "Hi, Amy. Hi, Lucia." She skipped saying hi to Fiona.

Mitchie ignored Fiona, too. "Hey, Amy — Jenelle, Kiwi, and I are going to see the new Ashley Violetta movie on Friday. It's playing at the Megaplex. Want to come?"

"Um, sure. Sounds great." My heart thrummed in my ears, and I couldn't decide if it was because I was happy to see my friends, excited to see the movie, or afraid that a fight was about to break out.

"Oh, too bad, Amy," Fiona said in a loud voice. "Because Lucia and I are going to a concert that night, and I was hoping you could come."

"We're going to a concert?" Lucia asked. She blinked blankly.

Fiona laughed loudly. "Oh, Lucia, I just love

how you say everything as if it's a question! Well, we've got to jet. See you at the Health-car-thingie, Amy!" And she traipsed off, Lucia following in her wake.

Jenelle watched them for a moment, then snorted. "Concert. Right."

Mitchie turned to me. "Why were you holding her hand?" she asked.

I held up the brand-new phone. "She gave me this."

Mitchie frowned at the phone, then at me, but Jenelle just squealed with excitement. "A Taffy!" she cried. "Now we can text each other!"

"What did she want in exchange?" Mitchie asked. "Your kidney?"

"It was just . . . a gift," I said.

"Nothing is ever 'just a gift' with Fiona," Mitchie said. "You always pay, one way or the other."

"That's not true," I said. But my voice sounded weak, even to me.

"We'll see," Mitchie replied.

I looked over at Jenelle, who was staring at the floor in silence. I wasn't sure if she wanted to defend Fiona and didn't dare . . . or if she wanted to warn me and didn't have the heart.

I guess Mitchie's right, I thought. *We'll see.*

CHAPTER TEN

Health Hint:
A human heart is the size of a fist. (Sometimes I wish I could use it as one.)

"Okay, what about if the kids just danced around however they wanted?" Fiona suggested later that day. "No game, just music and have a floor that lights up —"

"Anthony will pitch a fit," Preston said. "Forget it."

"Well, what about square dancing?" Fiona suggested. "I think I remember learning that once —"

"No dancing," Preston snapped. His voice was like a door slamming.

Fiona let out a frustrated sigh, and I sat at the smooth light wood library table trying to fight off a strong feeling of déjà vu. *Haven't I lived this exact day before?* I wondered as I stared out the window that overlooked the Allington golf course. *Except, last time, it was Fiona who kept shooting down Preston's ideas.*

Maybe Mitchie was right. Maybe it really is *opposite day.*

"Look, we have to do something cool for our final project." Fiona sat back in her chair and fixed Preston with her icy blue stare.

"We should just lecture the kids about exercise and hand out a brochure," Preston said. "Just do what Anthony wants and forget it." He leaned down to rub his ankle, which I could tell was still bothering him a little. His face was pale and he had dark circles under his eyes, and I wondered if the pain had kept him awake.

"Did you go to the doctor?" I asked.

Preston nodded, but he was looking down at the table. "He took an X-ray. It's just a sprain, but it still hurts."

"Why don't you take an aspirin or something?" Fiona suggested.

"I did," Preston replied. "It still hurts."

A minute passed. It was clear that none of us really knew what to say next. The silence was broken by an electronic chirping noise.

"Someone's cell phone is ringing," Preston said.

I looked over at Fiona, expecting her to whip one out of her purse. But instead, she just gave me this funny little smile. "I think it's yours," she said.

"Oh!" I pulled the phone out of my purse. "Sorry," I muttered as I touched a button. One text message, it read. I scrolled over the message and a name popped up: Jenelle Renwick.

MOVIE PLAYING AT CINEMA 21 — NEAR 5 MTNS. MEET FRIDAY AT 5:30?

Five Mountains was the big amusement park near the center of town. A new giant movie theater had just opened up a couple of months ago. Twenty-one giant screens with stadium seating.

My fingers floundered over the keyboard. I wanted to write: *Can't wait — this is going to be so much fun! Love! Amy!* But that would have taken me five hours to write, so I went with C U THEN.

"Sorry," I muttered again as I tucked the phone back into my bag.

Fiona just shrugged and got back to the topic at hand. "I don't want to do a lecture," Fiona said at last. Her voice was gentle, nothing like her usual sarcastic tone. "And I don't want to make a model of the human heart, and I don't want to hand out a brochure. Preston, you were right the other day. The best way to teach about exercise is to actually do some." She looked at Preston, then at me.

"But how can we do something creative when Anthony hates everything creative?" I asked. "Ms. Greene doesn't seem to mind. But she worships Anthony —"

"Well — does our final project actually have to be at the school?" Preston asked.

"I don't know," Fiona said slowly. "Our home-room teachers — not the volunteer advisors — are grading it, so . . . maybe not."

"So — you're saying that we could just do a health-and-exercise project," I said, "and it doesn't have to involve the Healthmobile?"

Preston nodded. "I think it just has to be about volunteering in the community."

"So — we could — we could, like, throw a party . . . and that could be our grade?" Fiona asked.

Preston rolled his eyes. "*No.* It has to involve health and volunteering."

"But what if . . . what if it was a party for the Allington community?" Fiona said, her words spilling out of her like confetti. "And what if it was a fitness party, where all of the games involved exercise?"

Preston looked doubtful. "Like what?"

"Like a moon bounce for people to jump on," I said. "Right?"

"And a basketball toss. And a stationary bike race," Fiona said.

"A three-legged race?" Preston suggested.

"And a sack race!" Fiona grinned.

"It'll be a field day." I felt the excitement pulsing through my arteries. . . . I swear, I think I even felt it in my ventricles. Wow. I guess I really *had* learned something about the circulatory system.

"Wait — we need to write these things down," Preston said. He flipped open his laptop and started to type.

"We can hold it at my house," Fiona offered.

I nodded. I'd been to her house once. The rear lawn was enormous — more than two acres in the middle of Houston. We could have an amazing party there. "Sacks for sack races don't cost very much," I said. "But where will we get the money for the moon bounce?"

Fiona's delicate hand fluttered like a butterfly. "Daddy will take care of it."

"We should have healthy snacks," Preston said as he typed. "Fruits and veggies."

"My mom and I have serious chopping skills," I volunteered. "We can handle that."

"And I can get some cool prizes," Preston said. "My aunt works for WorldFit."

"Awesome!" Fiona cried, and I nodded. WorldFit makes cool sporting goods and clothes. "This is going to blow everyone's mind! Okay — we only have a couple of days to pull this together. I'll get Jake to print up some flyers. And he can videotape the party. Then we'll submit the video for our final grade."

"Who's Jake?" Preston asked.

"My mother's personal assistant."

Preston looked at me with a tiny smile as if to say, *Fiona's mother has a personal assistant?* I had to look away to keep from laughing, but I couldn't stop the cool, bubbly feeling that sparkled through me. Finally, Preston had smiled at me. For the first time all day.

This opposite day was turning out to be pretty good. I had a cell phone. We had a project plan — we were going to throw an amazing party!

And there wasn't anything Anthony could do to stop us.

Friday night, I looked down at the smooth face of my new cell phone. It still wasn't ringing.

Is this thing working? I wondered. I touched the face and it lit up, ready for action. But I'd already left three messages and sent five texts. I didn't think it made sense to send more.

Kirk had dropped me off at the movie theater half an hour ago. Yes, you read that right. My brother had gotten his learner's permit, and Dad actually let him drive the minivan. Dad kept slamming his foot against the floor of the car, trying to hit the brake. Unfortunately, the brake was on the other side of the car — next to the accelerator, which Kirk kept hitting instead.

"I think I'll drive us home," Dad said once we reached the movie theater.

"No, it's cool, Dad!" Kirk grinned. "I think I'm getting the hang of this." He turned to me. "And I'm going to eat that last chocolate cupcake left over from dinner!"

"That cupcake is *mine*," I reminded him. "I'm saving it for when I get home."

"Who saves a cupcake?" Kirk demanded. "That's insanity. I'm eating it."

"You'd better not," I warned. "Or that cupcake will be your last."

"All right, nobody's eating anyone's cupcake." My father sighed and looked at me. "Should I come back to pick you up in a couple of hours?"

"Sure!" I said with a smile. "I'll just call you on my *new cell phone* and let you know when I'm done! See how convenient it is to have a *cell phone*?"

Dad shook his head. "I know I'm going to regret giving you this two-week trial period." My parents had agreed to let me use the phone for a little while. They said that as long as I didn't get addicted to it or expect them to pay for it, I could keep it.

"You won't regret it," I promised him.

"When can *I* get a cell phone?" Kirk asked.

"When you figure out a way to pay for it," Dad replied. "Okay, take us home, Driver. And feel free to take twice as long as you did getting here."

Kirk let out a huge belly laugh. "Dad, you're hilarious!" he said, a split second before he peeled out of the parking lot.

Since then, I'd been waiting in front of the movie theater, watching as people stood in line, then as the line moved slowly forward and disappeared into the cool, dark building. Then another line would form. Cars came and went in the parking lot, dropping off groups of kids or pulling into a space and releasing a couple. Over my right shoulder, the Five Mountains fireworks show had started. Colors exploded and rained stars in the darkening sky. A roller coaster *clink, clink, clink*ed to the top, then screams cut through the night as the train of cars whooshed toward the ground. People buzzed by me, talking eagerly about the movie they were going to see, or excitedly about the one they just came from. But none of those people were my friends.

I frowned at my cell phone. Naturally, Mitchie's and Kiwi's phone numbers weren't in there. Lucia had done the programming, and I never would have expected her to know those numbers. I hadn't had time to figure out how to program the phone myself, and I didn't have their cell numbers memorized. And they didn't have my number. I hadn't given it to them, because I wasn't sure my parents would let me keep the phone.

My stomach filled with a strange hollow sadness as I thought about my friends, together . . . without me. *Were they just having so much fun that they'd forgotten me? Didn't they care?*

Oh, that's dumb, I told myself. *Of course they care — there's just been some mistake. You misunderstood the time or the day or the place or something.*

I knew that this had to be true — that there must be some kind of logical explanation for why my friends weren't here. But it's one thing to know something, and it's another thing to *feel* it. And the way I felt was lonely and forgotten.

I pressed Jenelle's number again, but it went into voice mail after one ring. "The caller you are trying to reach is unavailable at this time," said the smooth robot answering voice. "Please leave a message at the tone."

I hung up before the beep. I didn't want to leave another message. What good would it do?

"Amy?" called a familiar voice.

I looked over, expecting to see Jenelle. But instead, Fiona waved and hurried to join me. Lucia was with her.

"Hey," I said, walking halfway down the concrete steps to join her. "What are you guys doing here?"

"We're going to Five Mountains," Fiona explained. "Are you waiting for Jenelle?"

"Waiting . . . and waiting. The movie started forty minutes ago," I admitted.

"Forty minutes!" Fiona cried. Her dark eyebrows crept toward each other in a frown. "You've been waiting here for *forty minutes*?"

I smiled, a little embarrassed. "Well, I got here early. I've been waiting for an hour and ten minutes."

"What?" Fiona shrieked. "Where is she? Did you call her?" She whipped out her cell phone.

"Don't bother," I said. "She's not picking up."

"You are, like, way too nice?" Lucia said. "I'd have left an hour ago?"

"I kept thinking that maybe I'd gotten the time wrong," I explained.

"No — Jenelle probably just flaked." Fiona's voice was bitter. "I'm annoyed for you."

"I don't think of Jenelle as flaky," I said slowly. Honestly, she'd never flaked on anything before. Not even when she was just meeting me at my locker.

"Are you kidding?" Fiona demanded. She looked like she wanted to add something, but she just bit her lip. "Look," she said finally, "why don't you come with us? We're going to ride some rides, eat some fudge, watch a concert. . . ." She said the last part in a singsong, like she was trying to tempt me.

"I don't know. . . ."

"Or you could just go home?" Lucia suggested.

"No way, you have to come with us. You're not allowed to spend Friday night moping on the couch." Fiona grabbed my hand. "I'm not letting you go until you say yes."

She looked at me with a clear blue gaze that seemed perfectly open and friendly, and I realized with a sudden jolt that this was why Jenelle had been friends with Fiona for so many years.

There really was another side to Fiona. A very sweet side.

Silver fireworks exploded in the sky, shooting ribbons of shimmering diamonds.

"Okay," I said at last. "Okay, sounds great. I just have to call my parents."

"Excellent!" Fiona said, giving my hand a squeeze. "Then tell them that you're spending the night at my house. That way we can set up for the party tomorrow!"

My heart nearly burst with shock. *Spend the night?* But Fiona was totally serious. She was even dialing my number for me on her phone. "Here," she said, holding it out.

I didn't know what else to do, so I took it.

"Hello?" Kirk said.

"Hey, Kirk — would you ask Mom and Dad if it's okay for me to go to Five Mountains with my friend Fiona? She invited me to spend the night, too."

"What happened to Jenelle?" Kirk asked.

"She never showed up," I explained.

"Oh, man!" Kirk crowed. "Dis-missed! Dis-regarded! Dis-eased!"

I rolled my eyes. "Would you just ask, please?"

"Dis-resp — okay, hold on." There was silence for a few moments, then Kirk came back to the phone. "Mom says it's fine to go to Five Mountains, but she wants to call Fiona's parents and talk to them before you spend the night."

"Okay," I said. I asked Fiona her number, then relayed it into the phone. "Would you remind Mom that she met Fiona's parents at the Save the Earth fund-raiser?"

"Dude, I am not your secretary," Kirk said.

"You can have the last cupcake," I told him.

"I'll do it — but because I'm a nice guy, not because of the cupcake."

"I'll make sure to write that down in my diary," I told him.

We hung up, and I turned to Fiona. "All set!" I told her.

"Great!" she said warmly. "Now let's go have some fun! Scream Machine first!"

"Um, I am not, like, going on the Scream Machine again?" Lucia informed her. "No, thanks?"

"Fine — Amy will come, won't you?"

"I love roller coasters," I said with a smile.

"Then it's fate we found you!" Fiona said, tugging at my hand and leading me toward the giant fake mountains that made up the entrance to the amusement park. As we walked toward the lights and rides, I wondered if Fiona was right — if it was fate that I ran into them. It certainly seemed like more than just coincidence.

Part of me wondered if the universe wanted me to be friends with Fiona. It was starting to look that way.

The hallway glowed with the kind of gray light that comes right before dawn as I made my way down Fiona's wide stairway. I'd crept out of her room as silently as possible, leaving Fiona and Lucia asleep in their beds. Fiona had two enormous beds in her room, plus a couch that folded out. Everything was comfortable and beautiful — all done in shades of blue and purple that looked like a stormy sea. And it was perfectly tidy in the way that things are when you have someone who cleans up after you. Spending the night at Fiona's wasn't like my usual sleepover experience — with a sleeping bag on the floor. It was more like staying in a fancy hotel.

I was sure there was some kind of bell I could ring to get room service or whatever to bring me a glass of water, but it seemed easier to try to get it myself.

Besides, it was bad enough when the housekeeper had made up the pullout couch for me the night before. I wanted to say "sorry" for causing her any trouble. But then I thought Fiona would think it was weird, so I didn't.

I tiptoed into the semi-dark kitchen and flipped on the light.

"Oh, hi," Fiona said. She gave me a slightly bleary smile from her place at the table in the huge bay window overlooking the yard. "I should have known you were an early riser, too."

I laughed, partly from the surprise of seeing Fiona there. I hadn't even realized that her bed was empty. "No way," I told her. "I'm just here to get a glass of water. Then I'm heading back to sleep."

"Sorry you got stuck with the foldout couch," Fiona said.

"It's more comfortable than my own bed," I told her truthfully. "Hey, where are the glasses?"

Fiona pressed her lips together and looked at the closed cabinets. "Um . . . over the sink, I think."

I pulled open the cupboard. Spices. "Guess again."

Fiona winced. "Over the blender?"

"That's bowls. You've never had to get your own glass of water before?" I teased.

"We don't eat at home much," Fiona admitted.

I pulled open the cabinets one by one until I found the glasses. "The answer is the one on the end," I informed her as I filled my glass from the tap. Looking for ice, I pulled open the freezer. "Wow — you're not kidding." The only thing in there was a box of low-fat ice-cream bars. I slid into the chair across from hers. "You should see *our* freezer. Something falls on my foot every time I open the door."

"Well, the fridge is full now, thanks to all of your cut-up fruits and veggies," Fiona said. She looked out the bay window at the empty lawn. "The moon bounce people are late."

"Seriously?" I asked, twisting to look at the clock on the gleaming steel microwave. "It's only six twenty-eight."

"Okay, they're not late *yet,*" Fiona admitted. "They're supposed to be here in two minutes. But if they aren't here . . ."

"Everything will still be fine," I told her. "Even if we have nothing but sack races, everything will be fine."

Fiona looked at me, then shook her head. "I hate parties."

"Uh — wha? *You?* You're, like, the Party Queen of Allington Academy."

She ran a hand through her silky black hair — which still looked perfect, even though she'd just woken up. "They stress me out."

I tugged at my ear, wondering if there was a problem with my hearing. "Are you serious? What's to be stressed about?"

"I don't know — maybe the moon bounce won't show up, maybe the veggies will taste weird, maybe nobody will have fun, maybe nobody will come —"

"Wow." I didn't know what to say, so I just said "wow" again.

Fiona laughed a little, then smiled shyly. "I don't even like *going to* parties, they stress me out so much."

The sky was turning rosy, and the clouds were lit with gold. The grass, smooth as a green carpet, sparkled with dew. It was going to be a beautiful day.

"Well, this party will cure you," I said at last.

"You think?" Fiona asked. "You really think it'll be perfect?"

"No, I think something will go horribly wrong. Something always does. But once you *know* that, you can just relax and enjoy it."

"I don't think I can just relax. I'll spend my time

waiting for the horrible thing to happen, wondering what I'll do when it does."

"I already know what you'll do," I said.

Fiona tilted her head slightly.

"You'll handle it."

"But what if nobody comes, Amy? I'll be humiliated."

I cocked an eyebrow at her. "Are you kidding?" *Aren't you supposed to be the Queen Bee of Allington Academy?* I wondered. "Why wouldn't they come?"

Fiona smiled, but she still looked sad. "I don't know if you've noticed, but some of my friends have gotten a little mad at me lately."

I sighed. "Yeah." There wasn't much I could say to that one.

She looked into my face with that intense blue stare. "I know I can be a little harsh sometimes."

Sometimes? I thought. But then I had a flash of the fun we'd had the night before. Fiona had wanted to go on every single ride at Five Mountains. She was fearless. We spent forever playing games on the Midway. Surprisingly, Fiona had incredible aim — she'd even won a giant stuffed dog. We'd gone to the Taffy Shack to watch them make candy. Then we got a box of fudge and sat beside the log flume ride, watching the fireworks. And Fiona had paid for everything. I knew her family was rich and all, but still. She didn't have to do it. "You can also be really fun," I told her. "Sometimes."

Fiona gave me a wry little smile. "Thanks. I think."

"Besides, you know I'm coming to the party. Lucia's coming. And we know Preston's coming. That's a party. I mean, just watching Preston on the moon bounce will be entertainment enough."

Fiona laughed. "You're a good friend, Amy Flowers," she said. She was looking down at her water glass, and she spoke so softly that I wasn't sure I'd heard her correctly. But when she looked up, the gratitude in her face caught me by surprise. I wanted to say something. Something meaningful, but not cheesy. I mean, Fiona wasn't my best friend or anything. But she wasn't all bad, either. I never got a chance to speak though, because just then there was a shuffling noise at the door.

"What's going on?" Lucia asked as she staggered into the kitchen. "Like, now we're all getting up at five A.M. to hang out?" She frowned at me as if I *must* be responsible for this insanity.

"Fiona and I were just talking about the fitness party," I explained. "But it looks like she has everything under control."

Fiona flashed me a grateful look.

"You guys are so lucky that you've got a decent final project for Step Out?" Lucia said. "I still have no idea what I'm doing?"

"Well, couldn't you make a special meal for the homeless?" I suggested.

Lucia rolled her eyes. "I've been doing that already? I need something new?"

"Why don't you have a fund-raiser?" Fiona suggested. "Like a bake sale or something?"

Lucia looked doubtful. "I don't really bake?"

"But you cook," I pointed out. "You could sell empanadas and burritos and stuff like that."

Lucia fiddled with the tips of her bouncy brown hair as if she was thinking it over. "But where would I sell it?" she asked. "It has to be someplace with a lot of people? And I don't want to just set up a table at school?"

An idea flashed into my mind. "There's this skate rally," I said quickly, remembering what Mitchie had said. "A ton of kids will be there. Maybe you could get a booth. And you could have information about the shelter, too, and maybe sign up some volunteers."

"Amy, that idea is genius." Fiona nodded as if the whole thing was settled.

Lucia looked at Fiona, then at me, as if she was taking something in. Her eyes narrowed a little, and for a moment I thought she might say that she didn't want to set up a booth. But she didn't. "Yeah, Amy," she said at last. "Like, great idea? You're always *so* helpful?"

"Oh, sure," I said, even though Lucia didn't really *sound* grateful. Still, I didn't care if she was lying. Sure, this whole conversation was a little *Twilight Zone*-y, and part of me wondered if it was taking place in a parallel universe. On the other hand, at least the League was being nice. So I had no reason to be mean, right?

It was time to just give peace a chance.

CHAPTER ELEVEN

**Health Hint:
Your mouth makes one to three pints of saliva a day. (You need it to eat burritos . . . and, you know, other stuff.)**

"Attention, everyone! Attention!" Fiona blared into the bullhorn. "The jump-rope contest will begin in five minutes! And the frozen fruit-pop stand is now open. We're giving away cherry, coconut, strawberry, and raspberry-lime flavors — don't miss out!" She flipped the OFF switch and turned to me as shrieks of laughter blasted from the moon bounce. "How was that?" she asked me.

"You know, usually when people don't think anyone will show up to their party, they don't bother buying a bullhorn," I pointed out.

Fiona smiled. "It pays to be prepared."

I had to admit, the bullhorn was a good idea — because the party was *packed.* It looked like almost everyone from our grade had turned up. People were into every game, and they'd already devoured a bunch of healthy snacks. Lucky for us, it was a clear day, not too humid. It felt more like late spring than like summer. In Houston, March can go either way.

Someone let out a whoop from the dance floor. Fiona had set up the holographic dance game. We'd appeased Preston by putting up a sign that read, FOR TALENTED DANCERS ONLY.

"This way, guys," Fiona said to the camera crew she'd hired to film the party. "Let's be sure to catch part of the water-balloon toss."

"Fiona, great party!" Voe Silk, the reigning dramarama of the eighth grade, called as she passed by, waving a raspberry-lime ice pop. The two friends with her nodded their approval. That was about as much as anyone could expect from the eighth graders, I guess.

"Excuse me! Excuse me! Fiona!" Anthony's face was so twisted with anger that it took me a full thirty seconds to recognize him. "Just what do you people think you're doing?" He waved a flyer in Fiona's face. "I found *this* at the Allington tennis courts. I hope you realize that this party is not sanctioned by the Health on the Move Experience!"

"Please get this out of my face," Fiona said calmly, nodding at the flapping flyer. "We're just throwing a party."

"Are you telling me that this isn't your final project?" he demanded.

"It's our project," I said. "But —"

"Your final project has to involve the Health on the Move Experience!" he screeched. "And this doesn't!"

"Exactly," Fiona replied. "It doesn't involve you, so why don't you just —"

"Tony!" Ms. Greene waved frantically as she hustled over to join us. "Tony, I had to park the car three blocks away. It looks like you health volunteers know how to get a great turnout! Tony showed me your flyer. I think this party is brilliant — just brilliant!"

Anthony ground his teeth. "But it isn't sanctioned by the Health on the Move Experience."

Ms. Greene blinked at him in surprise. "Does it have to be?" She turned to Fiona. "My dear, I'm sure you realize that we can't assume any liability whatsoever —"

"Absolutely," Fiona said sweetly. "It's just a fitness party. It doesn't have anything to do with you — except that we were inspired by your Health Experience."

Ms. Greene giggled, then stopped when she caught sight of the ice pops. "Oh, ice pops! Tony, sweetheart, I'll be right back. Great seeing you girls — toodles! Hope you get an A!"

I cast a glance at Anthony, who was looking at the ground.

"'Sweetheart'?" Fiona asked him.

"She's my mom," Anthony explained, a little shamefaced.

Fiona and I exchanged a look. *His mom?* No *wonder* he thought he owned the Healthmobile!

"Well, uh — well, I guess it's okay. . . ." he said at last. He cleared his throat. "Um . . . I guess I'll see you later?" He hurried off in the direction of the obstacle course.

"Have a nice health experience," Fiona muttered.

I caught sight of a familiar blond head near the smoothie table. Jenelle was chatting with Lucia. For a second, I wasn't really sure what to do. I mean, she'd stood me up the night before. *But she couldn't have done it on purpose, right?* I thought. *It must have just been some mistake.* I decided it was dumb to just stand there wondering what happened when I could just ask, so I walked up and tapped her on the shoulder.

Jenelle looked surprised to see me. Surprised, but not exactly thrilled. "Oh, hi," she said. Her voice was as cold as a raspberry-lime ice pop and her eyes were hard as she took a sip of her purple smoothie.

Lucia looked from my face to Jenelle's. "Um, I'm going to go check out the yoga field?" she said quickly. "I'll see you guys later?" She darted away, almost as if something was after her.

"Are you okay?" I asked. "I was a little worried about you."

"You sure know how to show it." Jenelle's voice was sarcastic — but it sounded kind of awkward on her. It wasn't her usual style.

"What?" I was a little confused. *Why is Jenelle acting so weird?* I wondered. *Maybe she really did mean to stand me up. . . .*

"Don't act innocent — you *ditched* us last night!" Jenelle finally blurted. "Mitchie, Kiwi, and I missed half the movie waiting for you! And then we called your house, and your brother told us that you'd gone off to Five Mountains with Fiona!" Tears brimmed at the edge of her eyes. "I can't believe you'd do that to us!"

My head was swimming. She started to walk off, but I grabbed her arm. "Wait — I didn't!" I cried. "You're the one who stood *me* up!"

Jenelle wheeled to face me. "What?" she shrieked. "You didn't even call to say you weren't coming!"

"But I *did* come!" I insisted. "I was waiting for you. Didn't you get all my voice mails and texts?"

"I only got one text — the one where you said you wanted to go to the big screen at Miller's Plaza."

"Miller's Plaza?" I repeated. That was on the other side of town from Five Mountains. "I never said I wanted to go to Miller's Plaza! You said you wanted to go to Cinema Twenty-one!"

Jenelle fumbled with her bag, finally pulling out her phone. She scrolled to the text and held it out to me. "Isn't this your name?" she demanded, pointing to the text.

I looked at the message. MOVIE WILL BE BETTER ON BIG SCRN AT MILLERS PLAZA, it read. MEET AT 6 UNDER BIG SIGN. Sure enough, my name had popped up with the message. "But that's not my phone number," I pointed out. I dug my phone out of my bag and scrolled to Jenelle's contact information. "Is your cell number 555-2012?" I asked.

Jenelle shook her head. "No."

"That's so weird. How could that happen?"

Her hazel eyes were wide, and suddenly, they narrowed. "She did it again."

"Who?" I asked.

"Fiona."

"Fiona? But . . ."

"This is exactly what she did to me and Anderson," Jenelle explained. "She reprogrammed my phone so that it looked like I was receiving a text from him, when it was really *her*."

"She wouldn't do that," I said. But my voice sounded lame, even to me.

"She *already* did it," Jenelle snapped. "She just did it *again*."

"No, I mean —" I wanted to say, "She wouldn't do that to *me*," but I couldn't force out the words. *Why on earth would you think that?* I wondered at myself. *Because she fooled you into thinking that you were her friend? Right. Fiona doesn't care about you. She never cared.*

The lump in my throat felt like a grapefruit on fire. I couldn't speak.

Just then, Mitchie came over. "Hey, where were you last night?" she asked, giving me a playful punch in the arm.

"Fiona pulled a trick on all of us," Jenelle said.

Mitchie shrugged. "I told you it was something like that. The minute Kirk said her name, I knew it."

"Attention, everyone!" Fiona's voice blared across the lush green lawn. "I hope you brought your swimsuits, because the pool relay is about to begin!" Her white, even teeth flashed as she laughed at something someone said. She caught sight of me and waved.

That smile burned me like hot oil.

"Excuse me," I said to Jenelle. "I've got to do something."

Mitchie took one look at my expression and said, "Smackdown," but I didn't even respond. I just stormed over to Fiona, who was giving Jake orders. "Make sure that the lifeguards are in their places before anyone even lines up for the relay," she said. "And then refill the smoothie cups — we're running low."

Jake gave her a mock salute. "Yes, ma'am." He turned to me and winked. "Hey, Amy. Great party, right?"

"Yeah. Thanks, Jake," I said. Normally, I would have liked to stop and chat with him — he was a really nice guy. But at that moment, my blood was simmering through my veins. I wanted to talk to

Fiona before something erupted. "Sorry — I just need to borrow Fiona for a second."

"What's up?" Fiona asked as Jake made his way toward the pool to check on the lifeguards.

"Let's walk," I said, wanting to get away from the chaos of the party. Suddenly, everyone's happy screeches and playful shouts were seriously working my nerves. "I need some quiet."

"Just let me tell the camera crew —"

"No, Fiona," I snapped. "Now."

Fiona looked surprised, but she didn't snap back. "Okay," she said softly, and followed me as I made my way to a far part of the property. We walked toward a stand of trees and a good-sized goldfish pond. I sat down on a stone bench at the far end, so that our backs were to the party. Fiona perched lightly beside me. After a moment, she shifted uncomfortably and cleared her throat.

"Are you — is everything okay?" she asked.

I knew my voice would wobble all over the place if I tried to speak, so I took a deep breath. Once I finally felt I could speak, I realized that I wasn't sure what I wanted to say. *Why are you so evil?* or *What is wrong with you?* popped into my mind, but what came out of my mouth was, "I thought we were friends."

Fiona nodded. "We are."

I looked at her. "No, we're not."

"What do you mean?" A little crease appeared between her perfect brows. "Of course we are."

"No, Fiona, we aren't. Because you don't even know *how* to be a friend." Suddenly, words were flowing from me like water from a faucet. "All you know is how to control people. How to manipulate people. Having friends isn't about having little robot slaves do whatever you want, all right?"

Fiona stared at me as if I'd slapped her. "Why are you saying this?"

"Why don't you tell me why I received a text message from Jenelle that Jenelle never sent?" I shot back, pulling the phone out of my bag. I held it up, pointing to the message. "Why don't you explain why someone told me to go to the wrong movie last night?"

"You think *I* did that?" Fiona demanded. "That wasn't me!"

"Oh, right! What — you're going to pretend that you've never pulled a prank in your life? You've never humiliated anyone? You've never *cut off their hair*?"

Fiona's face turned deep red. For a moment, she sat stock-still, as if she was frozen in place. Then, with a lightning-quick movement, she grabbed the phone from my hand and tossed it into the goldfish pond. It landed with a plop, and sank to the bottom. A large white-and-orange fish darted away with a start.

Fiona stood up and walked off.

Well, that was unexpected, I thought as I stared at the water. Rings were still spreading from the spot where the phone had landed. My simmering blood suddenly cooled, as if it had all boiled off and floated into the air as steam. I felt woozy and sick. I don't know what I'd wanted from Fiona. An apology, I guess. Tears. A confession. Regret. . . .

The pond blurred and swam. *Why am I crying? Fiona should be crying, not me!*

But that didn't stop the tears from coming.

"Hey, there you are!" Preston's cheerful voice called behind me. "Amy, I bet we're going to get an A-plus — the party is going —" He stopped when he saw my face, and his expression changed to concern. "Hey," he said gently. Then he came and sat down beside me.

He didn't ask me what was wrong, or even if I was all right. I guess it was pretty obvious that I wasn't. He just put an arm around my shoulders. It was as if someone had cut the strings holding me up. I sort of sank against him, and rested my head against the space between his neck and his shoulder.

We sat like that for a long time. Finally, I sighed a little, and Preston shifted his weight. "It's okay," he said gently.

A small breeze lifted the new leaves on the willow tree, and sun gleamed off the water. *It's okay*, I thought. *He's right; it's okay.*

"Thanks," I said finally. I swiped at the tears that had spilled down my cheeks.

Preston reached out and tucked a lock of hair behind my ear. His fingertips were warm where he brushed my neck. I'd never been this close to him before, and I noticed that his eyes held tiny gold-and-green flecks. My pulse throbbed in my temples.

"Amy —" Preston began.

A twig cracked behind us, and I turned just in time to see Scott standing there. He looked at me with those deep-brown eyes.

I stared into them, feeling paralyzed. I could feel Preston's gaze on my face. Part of me wanted to jump up and shout, "Preston's just my friend!" Another part of me wanted to hide.

But I didn't do either of those things, and the moment passed by. Scott didn't say anything, either. He just turned and walked away.

I snapped out of my trance. "Scott?" I called, but he didn't turn back. "Scott!"

"He didn't hear you," Preston said. "He's too far away." But he didn't sound like he believed it.

What did Scott see? I wondered. *What does he think?*

"Look, I've got to get back to the party," Preston said quickly. He brushed off his shorts as he stood up, and just like that, the spell was broken. "You're okay, right?"

"I'm fine," I told him, running a nervous hand through my hair. "Totally fine. Thanks!" I tried to smile, but I'm sure it looked as carved on as a jack-o'-lantern's. My brain was jumbled with about a thousand thoughts. *What just happened with Scott? What just happened with* Preston*? What was Preston about to say? Why did I care so much?*

And why wasn't I more worried about Scott? He's the one I'm crushing on, right?

I mean . . . right?

"Isn't this rally hot?" Mitchie asked as she watched a guy flip a triple three-sixty at the top of the pipe.

"Definitely," Anderson agreed, wiping the sweat from his forehead. "It's got to be ninety-five degrees out."

Mitchie laughed. "No, I meant — isn't it *great*."

"It's mind-blowing," Kirk said warmly. "I still can't believe I skated the pipe flawlessly!"

"You fell down three times," I pointed out.

"Yeah, but that was *after* I skated it flawlessly," Kirk replied. He swooped his hands in a U. "I went up, I went down, I went up —"

"You stayed down," I finished for him.

He shoved my shoulder playfully.

"I can't believe anyone can skate the half-pipe," Kiwi said, wide-eyed. "It looks terrifying."

"Nah," Mitchie said. "It's fun."

"Yeah, the way being chased by werewolves is fun," Jenelle said. "I'm with Kiwi — it's scary."

"Listen, I told Andy I'd meet him over by the street-skating." Kirk jerked his thumb over his shoulder, toward the skate park's rails and stairs. "Anyone want to join?"

"I'll check it out," Mitchie volunteered.

"Actually, I wanted to visit Lucia's food stand," Jenelle said. "She needs an A on her final project. Besides, all of the money is going to the soup kitchen."

"And she makes a killer empanada," Kiwi added with a laugh.

"Excellent! I'm starving!" Anderson beamed at Jenelle as if she had just come up with the most brilliant idea ever. "I love eating for a good cause!"

My stomach let out a low rumble. It was nearly two o' clock, and I hadn't eaten since breakfast. "I'm there. We'll meet you guys at the rails, okay?" I said to Kirk and Mitchie.

"Kirk!" said a warm voice. Alizae appeared behind Mitchie's elbow. She was looking gorgeous in an orange sundress. Her hair spilled over her shoulders in dark waves. "I should have known I'd run into you here!"

"Alizae!" Kirk looked surprised — and embarrassed. "Um, are you into skating?"

Alizae laughed as if that was the best joke she'd ever heard. "No way!" she cried. "But my cousin is on the Beak-13 Skate Team. I thought I'd come and cheer her on. Did I just overhear that you were headed over to the street rails? That's where I'm going."

"Oh, yeah, Mitchie and I were just about to —" He waved his hand.

"Actually . . . uh . . . I just realized that I'm starving," Mitchie said quickly. "I'm going to check out Lucia's food stall, too."

"Are you sure?" Kirk asked.

"Yeah," Mitchie said, turning pink. "Yeah, you guys head over. We'll meet you there."

"Great!" Alizae said brightly. "See you later!"

Kirk looked like he wanted to argue with Mitchie, but Alizae was already tugging at his hand. He tripped after her.

"Wow, that girl is gorgeous," Anderson said, watching Alizae walk off with Kirk.

"Anderson!" Jenelle punched him lightly on the arm. She flashed him a warning glare and shook her head.

"Not as gorgeous as any of you guys," Anderson added quickly. "But —"

"Come on, before you dig any deeper," Jenelle said, dragging him toward Lucia's stall.

Mitchie sighed, and Kiwi put a gentle hand on her back. I linked my arm through hers, and we walked slowly toward Lucia's stall. "Maybe Fiona had a point," Mitchie said after a while. "About guys thinking of me as one of them."

"Are we listening to Fiona now?" Kiwi asked.

"No way," I said. My skin burned at the mention of her name.

Mitchie hesitated. "No, but — maybe she was right."

"Mitchie!" I cried, pressing her arm. "You're beautiful, okay? And guys think you're awesome."

"Yeah, but —" She bit her lip.

"And Fiona is a lunatic," Kiwi put in as we neared Lucia's food stall. Anderson and Jenelle were standing at the counter while Lucia rolled up their burritos. "I still can't believe she pulled that trick on you, Amy."

Lucia's hair was twisted up in a chopstick, and I noticed a blush creep up her neck. I felt a little strange talking about Fiona in front of her — after all, they were still friends. . . .

Jenelle toyed with a lock of blond hair. "You know what's weird about it?"

"Um, the fact that I believed she was for real?" I asked. I couldn't help the bitterness in my voice.

"Well, that, too," Jenelle admitted. "But Fiona usually admits it when she pulls a prank. She likes to take credit."

"Yeah, Fiona's not a liar?" Lucia said as she handed over the burritos. "But you're not even being fair? What makes you think she pulled the prank?"

"Who else would pull it?" Mitchie asked.

"But Fiona would never tell Jenelle to go to Miller's Plaza?" Lucia added a few extra chips to Jenelle's plate. "That place is, like, Skanktown?"

There was a full second of silence, while Jenelle finished the bite of burrito she had taken. "How did you know that I went to Miller's Plaza?" she asked.

Lucia's smile froze. "What?"

"How did you know that I went to Miller's Plaza?" Jenelle repeated. "Unless Fiona told you."

"Oh, yeah." Lucia nodded. "I guess . . . um . . . I guess she did mention it? I just forgot?" She laughed nervously.

Jenelle's right eyebrow curved like a question mark, while an idea slowly took shape in my mind. . . .

"I need to get some more salsa from the truck?" Lucia giggled again and hurried away.

Jenelle and I exchanged a look. "Whoa," I said.

"I know —" Kiwi agreed, gaping at Anderson's empty plate. "Anderson — you just inhaled that burrito in twenty seconds!"

"I was hungry!"

"No," I said slowly, "I meant *whoa*."

"Major whoa," Jenelle agreed. "But how did she come up with —"

"She didn't have to," I said. "Fiona already did it once. All Lucia had to do was ask Fiona how she did it, then copy it."

Mitchie made the time-out signal with her arms. "Um, excuse me — what are we talking about?"

"Fiona didn't pull the prank," I explained in a whisper. "Lucia did."

"What?" Kiwi shrieked.

"It makes perfect sense," Jenelle explained, drawing us away from the food stall. "Amy was getting to be better friends with Fiona —"

Mitchie made a retching noise.

"— and Lucia got jealous," Jenelle went on, ignoring Mitchie. "She wanted to get rid of Amy, so she pulled the prank —"

"— knowing that I'd think Fiona did it," I finished.

We looked at one another.

"Wow, that's really — what's the word?" Anderson asked.

"Evil?" Kiwi asked.

"Smart?" Mitchie suggested.

Anderson shook his head. "No — that word that means both."

"Devious," I said.

"That's it." He sounded kind of impressed. I didn't blame him.

Mitchie snorted. "Great — I hope they stay best friends forever. They're perfect for each other."

I'd lost my appetite — but my stomach was still churning as we made our way over to the street-skaters. *So, does that mean that Fiona and I really* were *friends?*

I remembered how she'd been over the past few days. She'd seemed softer, as if her fight with Jenelle had made her think about treating people differently. She'd been treating *me* differently.

Should I apologize? An image of her face — the tears in her eyes, the hurt — flashed through my mind. *How could we ever be friends again now?* My head was buzzing, and my stomach felt tight. I'd told her that she didn't even know *how* to be a friend. *Can you take something like that back?* I wondered.

How?

It was so strange to think that all of the times I had trusted Fiona, I had been wrong. And then, the one time I *should* have trusted her, I was wrong again.

I looked around, wishing she would appear. If I ran into her, maybe I could apologize. But it was a skate rally, after all. Not exactly Fiona's type of entertainment.

When we reached the rails, Mitchie was ambushed by a small crowd of skaters, all begging her to hit the track. Kirk was standing with his friend Andy, cheering as a guy pulled an amazing grind down the full length of a waist-high rail.

"Hey — where's Alizae?" I asked in a low voice, hoping that Mitchie was out of earshot.

Kirk didn't tear his eyes from the action. "Oh, she ran into some friend of hers," he said.

"So, what's the deal with her?" I pressed him. I wanted to find out once and for all if Alizae was his girlfriend. I had to know — for Mitchie's sake.

"What does that mean?" Kirk asked.

"I mean — what's . . . uh . . . is she just a friend of yours?" I winced, hating how dumb that sounded. "Or is there — is there more to it?"

Finally, Kirk turned away from the skaters. "Are you trying to embarrass me or something?" he demanded in a low voice.

"No, I —"

"Isn't it *obvious*, Amy?" he snapped.

"Well, I just wasn't sure —"

"You're just dying to hear me say it, aren't you? Well, fine. You win, Amy!" He cupped his hands around his mouth and shouted, "Attention, world! Alizae Khan is Kirk Flowers's math tutor!" He dropped his hands. "Are you happy now?"

I looked over at Mitchie, who was staring at me, slack-jawed.

I shook my head, feeling as if my brain was rattling around in there. "She's your — what?"

"My geometry tutor, okay? Yes, I admit it! I need help in math. I'm not a genius like you." He folded his arms across his chest and turned back to watch the skating. "Thanks for throwing it in my face."

I couldn't help it — I reached out and hugged him.

"Hey, stop it," he said, trying to shake me off. But I was too strong. Finally, he just let out a sigh of surrender. "Man, you're weird sometimes."

I smiled over at Mitchie, who was grinning back. "Hey," she said suddenly. "I think I'm going to skate this course."

Kirk nudged Andy as Mitchie hustled to the starting point with her pink board. "Watch this," Kirk said. "That girl is amazing."

"Hey," Jenelle said, tapping me on the shoulder. "Someone is trying to get your attention."

It was Preston. He was waving at me from the soda stand. "Flowerdy Flowers!" he crowed. An electric thrill shot through me as he loped toward us.

"Hm." There was a twinkle in Kiwi's eye as she studied my face.

I hushed her just as Preston reached us. "Think fast!" he said, and in the next moment, something cold and slithery was sliding down my back.

I screeched. "Did you just put an ice cube down my back? I'm going to strangle you!"

"You'll have to catch me!" Preston called. "And my ankle is healed, so good luck!" He darted away, laughing.

Are you serious? I thought. I couldn't believe he'd done that to me after yesterday. He'd been so sweet! I'd really thought there was something there. Something between us. But there wasn't. *No way. No how. He drives me crazy.*

Why do people have to be so complicated? Mitchie is a tomboy, but she loves to fix hair. Fiona is mean, but she can be incredibly generous and fun. And Preston . . .

"Preston Harringford is the most annoying person on the planet," I griped.

Kiwi looked as if she was trying to swallow a smile.

"Hm," is all she said.

Don't miss Amy's next adventure at Allington Academy:

By Lisa Papademetriou

Another

Candy Apple book . . .

just for you.

coming soon from

Candy Apple . . .

Cassie Cyan Knight is back! The irrepressible heroine of *Miss Popularity* returns in a brand-new adventure about friendship, the great outdoors, and the perfect pair of hiking boots.